The mood shifted the moment Matt touched her.

Light flirtation was over. This was serious stuff. Ella tried to ignore his hand as he tucked the wayward strands behind her ear, but couldn't. A shiver ran down her spine, and she couldn't stop herself from leaning, just slightly, into his hand.

"You, Ella, are beautiful, smart, and can single-handedly organize large weddings." He brushed her bangs back off her face. His hand slid down so that he cupped her cheek. His eyes locked with hers. "That's impressive."

He was so close Ella could feel his breath and the warmth radiating off his body. His voice and the gentleness of his hand hypnotized her. He had called her beautiful. This unbelievably gorgeous man had called *her* beautiful. Her mouth went dry, and she swallowed hard—again—but still couldn't get her voice above a whisper. "I'd say you were the impressive one."

To illustrate her point, she laid one hand on Matt's broad shoulder, slid it down to where his biceps bulged under his shirt, and squeezed the hard muscle. She had meant to simply emphasize his size, but at her touch Matt's breath caught, and his hand reflexively curled around the nape of her neck to pull her closer to him.

Dear Reader

I once heard someone describe his ten-year marriage as a 'one-night stand that just got completely out of hand'. That lit my imagination. How could something so temporary and transient in its nature lead to a happily ever after? Could the intense spark of physical attraction that fuels a one-night stand really have staying power? So I took two characters who seemed likely candidates for a temporary arrangement—Ella, a commitment-phobic control freak, and Matt, a workaholic who lives in a different state—and let those sparks fly. THE SECRET MISTRESS ARRANGEMENT is the result.

Call me a hopeless romantic, but I love to fall in love. That's why I read romance. But I really love that I've found a career where I can do that over and over again—and hopefully give that feeling to readers as well. As my first couple to come to life in the pages of a book, Matt and Ella will always have a special place in my heart. I hope they'll earn a special place in yours.

All the best

Kimberly

THE SECRET MISTRESS ARRANGEMENT

BY
KIMBERLY LANG

First published in Great Britain 2009
This edition published 2010
Harlequin Mills & Boon Limited,
Eton House, 18-24 Paradise Road, Richmond, Surrey TW9 1SR

© Kimberly Kerr 2009

ISBN: 978 0 263 21028 6

Harlequin Mills & Boon policy is to use papers that are natural, renewable and recyclable products and made from wood grown in sustainable forests. The logging and manufacturing process conform to the legal environmental regulations of the country of origin.

Printed and bound in Great Britain
by CPI Antony Rowe, Chippenham, Wiltshire

Kimberly Lang hid romance novels behind her textbooks in junior high, and even a Master's programme in English couldn't break her obsession with dashing heroes and happily ever after. A ballet dancer turned English teacher, Kimberly married an electrical engineer and turned her life into an ongoing episode of *When Dilbert Met Frasier*. She and her Darling Geek live in beautiful North Alabama with their one Amazing Child—who, unfortunately, shows an aptitude for sports.

Visit Kimberly at www.booksbykimberly.com for the latest news—and don't forget to say hi while you're there!

**This is Kimberly's debut novel
for Mills & Boon® Modern Heat™!**

To my wonderful husband Peter.

Thank you for believing I could do this
and for your unwavering support while I did.

I'm very lucky to have you…

CHAPTER ONE

"DAMN, damn, damn!"

Matt leaned on the horn as a Cadillac swerved into his lane without indicating and slowed to about twenty-five miles an hour. He was now over an hour late for the wedding rehearsal, and at this rate he was going to miss the dinner, as well. In Matt Jacobs's world, only idiots showed up late, and he didn't like to be one.

He accelerated around the Caddy but suppressed the urge to flip the driver off. How could getting to a wedding be so difficult? Getting to Chicago from Atlanta should have been easy. But, *no*. Instead, a last-minute client meeting caused him to miss his flight out last night, and bad weather canceled or delayed all outgoing flights this morning. The resulting chaos at Hartsfield airport as the airlines reshuffled put him at O'Hare without even enough time to grab a shower before fighting the traffic out to the church in his old stomping grounds of Berwyn.

His cell phone rang. Glancing at the number, he

contemplated ignoring it. He was on his first real vacation in three years, after all. Instead he answered the call on hands-free and barked instructions at the paralegal at the other end.

Swinging the rental car into a parking space at the church, he could see the caterer carrying food into the parish hall behind the sanctuary. At least he was still in time for dinner.

"Look, make the changes they want. It's not a real problem. Just be sure to run the contract by Darren to double-check before anyone signs it. You all will have to handle this without me. I'll check messages on Monday, but I'm turning my phone off now." He tossed the phone into the glove compartment for good measure. He'd been accused of being a workaholic before, and it had served him well so far, but even he had his breaking point. They could damn well get by without him for a week.

The October breeze felt good after a day spent in airports and airplanes, but the nip it carried promised winter was not far behind. Grumbling, he grabbed his jacket from the backseat. He'd traded frigid, snowy winters for hot, sunnier climes years ago and never regretted it.

When he entered the church, he could see Brian surrounded by his family, playing the part of happy groom to the hilt, and several of his high-school friends milling about. He forgot about his disastrous afternoon as Brian caught his eye and waved and Jason, another of their childhood friends, approached Matt with a large grin.

"You made it. I was starting to wonder."

"Me, too." Matt ran a tired hand through his hair, wishing again he'd had time for a shower. "Did you pick up my tux?"

"It's at Brian's."

"Thanks. How mad is Brian that I missed the rehearsal?"

"Oh, he's fine about it. It's Ella who's spitting fire." Jason nodded toward a group of women surrounding the bride.

"Who?"

"The maid of horrors. I'd steer clear if I were you." Jason paused as a woman carrying a clipboard separated herself from the group and headed in their direction.

Oh, *that* Ella. In the three years Brian had been dating Melanie, he'd heard about her, but their paths had never crossed before now. "I think she'll——"

"Too late. Someone's told her you're here. See ya." Jason practically ran toward the other groomsmen, who called out greetings but made no attempt to come over and say hello to him.

Watching Jason hightail it away was strange enough, but the others' attitudes were equally odd. What was that about? Matt turned his attention to the young woman purposefully approaching him, her high heels tapping on the stone floors.

She was petite, almost tiny really, but perfectly formed for her height. Silky dark hair brushed her shoulders and called attention to her fair skin. In a pale-blue dress that clung in all the right places and seemed to float around her shapely calves, she hardly looked like a harridan who would send Jason skittering off to the safety of the other groomsmen. As she got closer, he could see that what would have normally been a very pretty face was pinched with stress.

"I'm Ella, Melanie's maid of honor. You're Matt, right?"

So much for the polite formalities. With a smile meant to charm, he extended his hand to her. "Matt Jacobs, best man, reporting for duty, ma'am."

"Great." The word had zero emotion behind it, and she shook his hand absently. "We were worried that you wouldn't make it at all tonight." She had yet to actually look at him directly, and he found himself wondering what color her eyes were. She remained focused on the clipboard in front of her and consulted it as she talked. "David Parks stood in for you at the rehearsal. You'll need to get with him so that he can show you where to go and what to do. We don't have time to walk through it all again, but David and Brian can probably tell you everything you'll need to know. If you have any questions, come talk to me."

She had a soft, almost husky voice that clashed with her size, but her tone was all business. And, unless he was losing it, he was hearing a drawl that said she wasn't native to the area. "Let's see, after dinner, Father Mike wants to meet with you and the other groomsmen in his study, so don't disappear. Now, did someone pick up your tux for you?"

Ella may have been pocket-size, but she was for-midable. No wonder Jason ran at her approach. All Matt could do was nod as she jumped from topic to topic.

"Good." She actually checked something off on the list in front of her. "Be sure to try it on tonight to make sure it fits. Check you have all the shirt studs and cuff links as well. If there are any problems, call the shop in the morning, and they'll make arrangements for you to come in. Here's the number." She handed him a business card. Pausing, she looked him over carefully, eyes nar-rowed, and he had the uneasy feeling he was being in-spected for something. Whatever she was looking for, he guessed he passed, because she nodded and checked something else off her list. "Now, I need to talk to you about the bachelor party. I assume you have something planned for this evening—"

Matt interrupted her with a laugh. "Don't worry. I already told Melanie that I wouldn't lead Brian astray or—"

"I don't care what y'all do." Surprise and disbelief must have shown on his face because she waved a hand dismissively. "Seriously, I don't. All I care is that you have Brian at this church, bright-eyed, bushy-tailed and ready for pictures by one o'clock. Understand?"

She finally looked directly at him with her last statement. Wide green eyes held a "Don't mess with me" warning, and silent agreement seemed the safest course of action.

"Good. Make sure the other groomsmen understand

that, as well. I don't want any bleary, half-drunken men coming in late and unshaven." Consulting her clipboard one last time, she seemed satisfied and attempted a smile that fell flat when it didn't reach her eyes. "I know Brian is looking for you, so I'll let you go find him." A cell phone Matt hadn't seen earlier rang, and Ella juggled the clipboard to her other hand as she retrieved it. With an "Excuse me" she was gone, already engrossed in conversation with whoever was on the other end.

Clearly dismissed, he watched her walk to where the caterers were setting up for dinner, obviously unhappy about something and consulting her clipboard as she went.

With Ella's departure, Jason returned to his side. "I told you so."

He understood now why Jason and the other grooms-men were staying far away. "Good Lord, I haven't been talked to like that since Sister Mary Thomas called me into her office in tenth grade after the girls' locker room had been raided."

"Exactly." A bitter and exasperated tone edged Jason's voice. Ella must have really given him a hard time about something. "Hell, she lined us all up earlier, checking to see if we needed haircuts."

So that's what the inspection was about.

"Well, she made an appointment for me to get a haircut *and* called to make sure I went." Brian had finally disengaged himself from his family and joined the group surrounding Matt. Brian greeted his oldest and best friend with, "So for once *you're* the idiot."

"I know, I'm sorry. The airline canceled—"

"No problem." Brian's good-natured shrug was a nice contrast to Ella's earlier reaction. "It's not all that complicated a job. Stand, walk, hold the ring. You're a smart guy—I think you can handle it."

"I'm not sure Ella agrees with you."

"Ella? She knows you'll have it under control. Melanie and this wedding have her wound a bit tight these days, but Mel would be a complete basket case by now without her. She's done an amazing job."

"Well, I don't know much about her, but she's certainly missed her true calling."

Brian nodded. "Yeah, I've been telling her for weeks now she should open her own bridal consulting business."

"I was actually thinking drill sergeant. Or maybe one of those nuns from high school."

"Ella? A nun? Hardly." Brian laughed. "We call her Melanie's attack Chihuahua. Tiny, but fierce when crossed. You might be onto something with the drill sergeant thing, though." He inclined his head toward his groomsmen. "She certainly has this motley crew toeing the line."

Matt looked over to where Ella had reestablished herself by Melanie's side, cell phone and clipboard held unobtrusively behind her back. Whatever the crisis had been, it was either averted or solved, and Ella was all smiles as she talked to Melanie and her family. The pinched look was still there around her eyes, but she certainly no longer looked quite so formidable. In fact, she looked…

No, Ella wasn't nun material. Hiding that body under a nun's habit would be a crime. He watched as Ella answered her cell again, and her expression changed from serene to agitated as she read the riot act to the poor fool on the other end. This was going to be one interesting wedding.

Melanie's wedding day dawned bright and beautiful, and Ella spent the day with her at the local spa being massaged, manicured, coiffed and pampered—in between phone calls concerning minor and major wedding emergencies. She'd intentionally booked Melanie's treatments opposite hers so the incoming calls would not distract or worry Melanie on her big day, but Ella had her hands full. She dealt with the caterer's problems during her pedicure and the florist's glitch during her massage. Brian's mother called twice during her hair appointment, frustrating both Ella and the stylist. Tension set in to muscles only recently kneaded, and a headache pulsed behind her eyes. She felt like she was the only person to ever leave a spa treatment more stressed than when she went in.

But, as she sat at the head table during the reception watching Melanie and Brian's first dance, she knew it had all been worth it. Melanie's wedding was everything they'd hoped for. Melanie glowed with happiness as she smiled at Brian and leaned in close to him. They made a stunning couple—both tall, blond, perfect people—and they were very much, very obviously to everyone, in love.

Ella couldn't have been more pleased. Or tired. Her face ached from smiling; her hand was limp and slightly bruised from shaking hands with a hundred guests in the receiving line. She was bone-weary from the past weeks of planning, organizing and keeping Mel calm and happy. All right, she'd admit there was a teeny-tiny bit of envy in there, too, but Mel was so blatantly happy, *anyone* would be envious.

At times like this, she wanted to believe in the fairy tale, the white picket fence and the happily-ever-after. Not that she knew very many people who actually made it work. Her parents had been, as Melanie kindly called it, too "free-spirited" to commit to anyone or anything, preferring free love and the call of the road. Even her grandparents hadn't managed it. In the end, they'd loved her, but not each other anymore.

But Mel believed it, and Brian knew that a failure on his part to deliver would be a death sentence. Not that she'd needed to make that threat. Melanie was the center of Brian's universe. Anyone could see that.

Lucky Melanie. Guys like Brian weren't exactly thick on the ground, though. She had a string of failures to prove it. Not that she was blameless, as Melanie reminded her all too often, but some people just weren't designed to do the whole my-one-and-only-soul-mate thing.

She was one of them. Bad genes, probably.

Maybe it was exhaustion, or possibly that fifth glass of champagne, but either way, she was getting just a tiny bit maudlin. That had to explain this need to navel gaze in the middle of Melanie's reception.

Emotion plus champagne equaled weepiness, so she forced herself to concentrate simply on the success of the moment. She could obsess over everything else tomorrow. Once Mel and Brian said their goodbyes, she was going home and going to bed.

Sleep. Sleep was all she needed to get everything back in perspective.

As other couples joined the bride and groom on the dance floor, Ella felt a hand on her shoulder and turned to find Matt Jacobs standing behind her chair. He held out a hand to her.

"Would you like to dance?"

It took a second for his question to register. One eyebrow arched up in response to her silence and she swallowed her shock. "I'd love to."

Placing his hand at the small of her back, Matt steered her toward the dance floor, and every nerve ending jumped to full alert. Although she'd been too busy last night to pay much attention to him, her proximity to him today had made it impossible for her *not* to notice him.

Melanie always described Matt as a cutie, but Ella decided he was really in the drop-dead-gorgeous category—particularly in his tuxedo. And he was *huge*. The cut of the tux just seemed to emphasize his wide chest, broad shoulders and lean waist. All day she'd felt like a midget just standing next to him—even in heels, she barely reached his shoulders—a feeling not helped by the constant fussing of the photographer as he tried to line them up for photos.

Matt's size had one benefit, though—he had no problem moving through the crowd. For once she didn't feel as though she was trying to fight her way through blackberry bramble. Instead folks just magically seemed to move out of the way.

As Matt pulled her into his arms to dance, Ella tilted her head back to look him in the eye. *Chocolate.* She'd read about men with chocolate-colored eyes, but she'd never met one who actually deserved the adjective. Ringed by lashes any girl would die for, those eyes had the power to turn her insides to mush. Mel's "cutie" classification seemed a woeful understatement.

When did it get so warm in here?

They made small talk over the music, with Matt having to practically bend himself in half to get close enough to hear her. Each time he did, though, her pulse spiked.

For such a big man, he moved with grace and ease. Ella's experience with men who could actually dance was very limited, but here was one who could not only dance, but knew how to lead properly as well.

"You keep surprising me, Matt."

"In good ways, I hope."

"Oh, definitely." All day long he'd been Johnny-on-the-spot, graciously assisting Mrs. Chryston to a chair off the aisle when her enormous bulk wouldn't squeeze into the antique pews of the church, or listening politely to Great-

aunt Elaine's long-winded story of Melanie's first commu-
nion without correcting her when she called him by the
wrong name. He even adeptly solved a minor crisis with
the limo service before she could even get to the scene.

He'd certainly done his duty as best man—and then
some. She owed him big-time. She also owed him an
apology. She cringed as she remembered the horrible
way she'd talked to him the night before.

She tried to keep her voice light. "I want to apologize for the way I acted last night…and today. I've been
kind of stressed the past few days, and I've been a bit,
um, snappish with people."

Matt cocked that eyebrow at her again and teased, "Is
that what you call it? Snappish?"

"In polite society that's what I'm calling it." Grateful
he wasn't going to hold a grudge, she relaxed into the
conversation. "I know what the groomsmen are calling
it when they think I'm out of earshot."

"You heard that?"

"Uh-huh. Feel free to let them know that I don't
consider 'control freak' to be an insult."

"What about your 'hair-trigger temper'?"

"If they'd act like adults, they wouldn't have to worry
about my temper."

He laughed, and the deep rumble moved through her
veins like strong coffee—warm and comfortable with
enough of a kick to make her blood pump. "You certainly have them running in fear."

"Well, for the most part, they deserve it. Particularly

that Jason." Her mouth twisted before she could stop it. "I know he's a good friend of yours, but I swear that boy is completely useless." She looked over to the bar where Jason had permanently stationed himself for the night and was currently chatting up one of the other bridesmaids.

Matt's gaze followed hers and he shrugged. "That much I'll give you. He's a nice guy, though. Worthless, but basically harmless."

"If you say so. I really expected Brian to have a more mature group of friends—present company excepted, of course." He nodded at the backhanded compliment, and she continued with a smile. "But I *am* sorry for the way I treated you. You didn't deserve it." For some reason she couldn't explain, it was important he realize she wasn't normally a shrew.

"Apology accepted, but it's not really needed. Brian's raved about how you really went above and beyond." He paused before looking at her questioningly. "Why?"

That caught her off guard. "Why what?"

"Why were you running the wedding? It seems strange that Melanie would put all the work on you when she could have easily hired a professional to do it."

"Best-friend duty, you know." At his skeptical look, she searched for the right words. "I want Mel to be happy. Whatever she wants, I want her to have. She wanted this wedding to be perfect, so I was determined to do whatever I had to in order to make it perfect for her. And she's having a good time, so I'm happy."

"And you? Are you having a good time?" Matt's

thumb stroked lightly over the skin of her back exposed by the deep halter cut of the dress, and Ella couldn't concentrate on the conversation. Every nerve in her skin seemed alive and attuned to him. *God, he even smells good.* Not in an I-bathed-in-my-aftershave kind of way, but a clean, slightly spicy and very masculine way. Each time she inhaled, the scent of him coiled through her and set her pulse to pounding.

She swallowed hard, trying to pull her concentration back to the conversation and away from the totally inappropriate thoughts whirling through her. "Of course. It's really been a beautiful wedding. I'll tell you though, as soon as Mel and Brian leave, I'm headed home to crash. I haven't had much sleep lately."

"I understand. I was out late last night myself. You know, strippers and hookers and such." He winked at her.

"I don't care, and I *really* don't want to know," she reminded him with a laugh. The music ended, and the bandleader announced the garter and bouquet toss. As Matt led her off the dance floor, she remembered something.

"Brian said that you're staying at his place while you're in town." At his nod, she continued. "I have some wedding presents at our apartment that I need to drop off. Would tomorrow afternoon be okay? I have a key, but I don't want to barge in on you, so I'll call first."

"I'll be at my mother's most of the day tomorrow, so any time is fine."

Ella nodded because she knew through Melanie that he had plans for the day. But his next words floored her.

"How about you let me take you to dinner tomorrow night? I'll take the presents back to Brian's after and save you a trip."

"Dinner?" Had she heard him correctly?

"Dinner."

She was still confused and obviously looked it.

"You know, that meal people eat late in the day? Come on," he coaxed, "you did a fantastic job with this wedding. Let me take you out to celebrate."

Where had this come from? "Um, okay…" Realizing she sounded reluctant, she stopped and slapped a smile on her face. "I mean, that sounds great."

"All right, then. Seven o'clock?"

She nodded, sensible words still escaping her.

"Is Salvador's okay with you? I haven't been there in ages."

Salvador's was a swanky place close to the South Pond, frequented by the young, beautiful and terminally hip crowd. Ella rarely went there, as she considered herself completely unhip. But the food was great, and if anyone would fit in with the crowd there, it would be Matt. Finally she managed another nod. *Great, he's going to think I'm a bobble-head doll.*

"I'll pick you up at seven."

"Okay."

With a smile and a small wave, Matt disappeared into the crowd. Without him to clear the path, Ella had to fight her way to Melanie. Her mind spun. Matt Jacobs wanted to take her out to dinner? *Why?* She could understand if he didn't know anyone else in Chicago, but he'd grown up here. His friends and family were here—many of them in this very room. Surely there were plenty of people for him to go out with. So why her?

Confusion, though, couldn't outrun vanity. To go to Salvador's with a piece of eye candy like Matt wasn't an opportunity that came her way every day. Since she was leaving Chicago next week anyway, it wasn't an opportunity likely to ever happen again.

What on earth would she wear?

She shook her head at her own silliness and continued to fight her way out of the mob.

Melanie was looking for her and pulled her into a tight hug as soon as she made it to her side. "Thank you so much for everything." Her voice caught, and her eyes misted.

"Don't you dare start crying," Ella pleaded as her eyes began to burn. "Your mascara will run."

"Screw my mascara. Everything has been so perfect today, and I—" Her voice broke this time, and Melanie paused for a deep breath. "I can't stand it that you won't be here when I get back. I'm so worried about you being all the way down south without anyone at all." Melanie managed a short laugh through her tears. "Heck, I'm worried about me—who will I talk to?"

"There's this wonderful invention called the telephone, you know." A sniff escaped, and Ella fought to keep herself together. "Anyway, I'll be back to see you at Thanksgiving. And Christmas. And every other minor holiday, too." Ella knew she was seconds from bawling her eyes out. "We've covered all this already."

"I know. I'm just going to miss you so much." Mel drew in a deep shuddering breath. "I love you, El."

"I love you, too. Now, go. Everyone's waiting for you to toss the bouquet."

"I want you to be the one who catches it. It's time for you to settle down now. Enough of this messing around. Promise me you'll catch it."

"I'll try," she lied.

Melanie stood on the steps leading out of the hall and turned her back to the crowd. As soon as she did, Ella stepped out of the mosh pit of single women jockeying for position and tried to slip to the sidelines, out of the way.

"One, two, three!" the crowd chanted, and Melanie heaved the bouquet over her shoulder.

But she threw it too high. Instead of flying directly into the waiting crowd, it caught one of the ceiling fan blades and was thrown off course, slicing neatly to the right, away from the mob. Ella looked up in time to see the bouquet headed straight for her. Reflexively, she caught it before it hit her smack in the face. The crowd cheered, and Melanie applauded before she was whisked away into the waiting limo, leaving Ella to face the aftermath alone.

Damn, she thought, as her taxi stood idling where the limo had recently been. *So much for early exits.* She spent the next hour receiving congratulations and pre-dictions about the lucky groom-to-be. To add insult to injury, that worthless Jason caught the garter, and she was forced to pose with him for photo after humiliating photo. More than once she saw Matt watching her, an amused smile playing around his mouth.

By the time she got home, she was too tired to do more than slide out of her bridesmaid's dress, leaving it in a puddle of navy silk on the floor, and fall headfirst into bed. Her last thought before exhaustion claimed her was that she still had no idea what she would wear the following night.

CHAPTER TWO

THE doorbell rang promptly at seven, and Ella wasn't ready. Between sleeping most of the day away and the fact her apartment was complete chaos, the simple act of getting dressed for dinner had taken on farcical properties.

Forced to choose between leaving Matt standing on the front steps or answering the door half-dressed, she padded down the stairs to the door, cinching her robe tightly closed as she went.

"Hi, Matt."

Whatever he was about to say in greeting died as his gaze swept her from head to toe, taking in her state of undress. Was it her imagination, or did his eyes seem to linger overly long on her legs, exposed by the thigh-length robe? He cleared his throat and looked at her quizzically. "Um, am I early?"

"No," she said, suddenly very aware of how little she was actually wearing. "I'm running late. Just give me a couple of minutes, though, and I'll be ready to go. Would you like to come up?"

It was a ridiculous question, as there was no place else for him to wait. While the entry was street level, her apartment was on the second floor of the brownstone. Short of having him sit on the steps, she had to invite him up.

At his nod, she led him up the stairs, belatedly realizing that the shortness of her robe was most likely offering him an unobstructed view of her bottom. She could feel the heat rushing to her cheeks. Probably *both* sets were blushing. Inwardly she groaned. This evening was already off to a bad start.

"Would you like a glass of wine or something?" He declined, so she continued. "Sorry the place is such a wreck. Between the wedding and the packing, everything is upside down. Try to make yourself comfortable, if you can, and I'll be ready in a minute." She offered him a half smile and disappeared through one of the doors leading off the living room, leaving it slightly ajar.

Matt tried to compose himself. He'd been knocked off guard when she'd opened the door, and was still recovering from the sight of Ella in that robe. The thin fabric had outlined every curve, clinging to the swell of her breasts. The tightly cinched belt emphasized her tiny waist and the flare of her hips. His eyes had avidly traveled down to the hem that skimmed the top of the most amazing legs he'd ever seen. Firm thighs, muscular calves and ridiculously trim ankles had him thinking that perhaps he was a Leg Man after all. But he changed his mind when she led him up the stairs and he'd been treated to a view of a beautifully shaped derrière clothed only in a thong. He'd been very glad when she left the room, giving him a chance to regain a sense of composure before he made an complete fool of himself.

He still wasn't completely sure what he was even doing at Ella's apartment. The invitation to take her to dinner had popped out of his mouth just seconds after it had popped into his head. It seemed perfectly natural at the time: dance with the pretty woman, flirt with the pretty woman, ask the pretty woman to dinner. He'd been as surprised by her answer as she'd been at his question. But he had to admit Ella intrigued him. From drill sergeant to blushing bridesmaid to half-naked temptress, she was quite the puzzle.

A puzzle with one hell of a nice behind, though.

Drawing a deep breath, he looked around the room, trying to pry his mind away from the image of a half-naked Ella in the next room. Empty boxes were piled in every corner, while full boxes marked with either an *E* or an *M* were neatly stacked against the far wall. Ella hadn't been kidding when she called the place a wreck.

"Are you both moving out?" he called into the next room.

"Yeah, it's crazy, isn't it? With the wedding and everything, we're a bit behind on the packing. It's frustrating, but now that the wedding's done, I should be able to get something accomplished." She laughed. "I'd better, because the moving truck will be here on Friday."

"Where are you moving to?" He could hear her in her bedroom—shuffling noises mostly, with the occasional muttered curse as she either dropped or tripped over something.

"Sweet home Alabama. Specifically, Fort Morgan, where I grew up. It's down on the Gulf Coast, about three hours east of New Orleans."

"So you *are* a Southern girl. I knew I heard a drawl."

"I know. Even after ten years, people know I'm not from around here the second I open my mouth. It catches them off guard, and it's kinda funny to see them react."

He heard a muffled thump, followed by another string of muttering. "Take your time. There's no hurry. Why are you going back to Alabama?"

"I've accepted a job with a company in Pensacola, actually, and it's just across the state line. It's an easy commute, and I can still live on the beach."

Unable to sit calmly, thanks to a raging erection, he wandered around the room, taking in the framed prints and canvases on the walls, hoping to distract himself. Ella, or maybe it was Melanie, had good taste in art. Nothing so mainstream as to be a cliché, but nothing too out there, either. Everything was edgy enough to be interesting, and the pieces made a tasteful and eye-catching collection.

Leaning against the wall, obviously demoted from wall space, based on the dust on their glass, were Melanie's and Ella's college degrees. Curious, he pulled Ella's out for a look.

There was a BS from Northwestern, and a master's

from the University of Chicago, both in computer science and both awarded to Ella Augustine Mackenzie. *Augustine?* Heck of a name to be saddled with.

Computer science. That seemed a bit odd, because Ella didn't really strike him as a computer geek. He looked around for evidence to the contrary. A table in the corner held a laptop, but it looked like any other laptop—nothing fancy or complicated. People who spent that amount of time in college studying CS didn't flip burgers, that's for sure, but Ella just didn't fit the usual mental picture.

Drill sergeant, wedding planner and now computer geek. Ella was full of surprises.

Chuckling as another loud thump—followed by a muffled curse this time—echoed from the next room, Matt wandered over to the bookshelf where Mel and Ella had a collection of framed pictures. There were snapshots of Brian and Mel on the beach somewhere, as well as a more formal pose he recognized as their engagement photo. There were many pictures of college-age Mel and Ella—group shots at parties, one of the two of them in front of a Christmas tree and another of them dressed to go to some kind of formal dance. He found family pictures of Mel and her brothers and parents. Ella was in most of the casual shots of Christmas and birthdays. He finally noticed a picture of a teenage Ella, braces and all, posed with an older couple to whom she bore a slight resemblance.

"Those are my grandparents."

Matt jumped as she spoke from directly behind him. He turned and lost the ability to speak. His mouth went dry, and he swallowed hard at the sight. The robe was gone, replaced by a dark-blue dress that skimmed over the curves of her body. Her shoulders and neck were bare, but she carried a sparkly wrap in one hand. The short dress and high heels only accentuated the incredible legs he'd seen earlier. All those remarkably erotic thoughts he had worked to cast out of his head returned full force.

Ella seemed completely unaware of his reaction to her as she leaned in to take the photo he still held in his hand. As she moved close to him, he caught a whiff of the perfume she wore—a light, but slightly musky, scent—and the erection he had only recently gotten under control began to stir to life again.

"I was sixteen when that picture was taken. My really bad hair aside, it's one of my favorite photos of us."

Matt struggled for something intelligent he could say as he tried to get the blood flowing back to his other head. He settled for, "Do they still live in Alabama?"

"No." Ella shook her head. "Gran died when I was in high school, and Gramps passed about five years ago." She smiled at the people in the picture fondly.

"And your parents? Are they still down there?"

"My parents both died when I was very young. My grandparents raised me." She didn't sound sad, only resigned, like someone who'd come to terms with the loss long ago.

Belatedly he remembered Melanie mentioning that to him before. Unable to think of anything less lame to say, he settled on, "I'm sorry."

She nodded and placed the picture back on the shelf where he'd found it. "Are you ready?"

"Ready." He cleared his throat. "You look fantastic, by the way." He was pleased to see that his ability to talk sensibly was coming back. "Well worth the wait."

Salvador's was still the place to see and be seen, and Ella got more than one envious glance from the other women there. Matt just seemed to attract stares from beautiful women, but, to his credit, he did nothing more than return an uncommitted smile. He proved early on he was more than just arm candy and a nice guy: he was a charming and fun date, as well. Their table had an amazing view, situated so neither of them had a back to the window. The chairs were close enough to each other to create an intimate feel while still giving them room to eat.

They ate ridiculously fattening food and talked easily about the wedding and people they both knew. It was, she realized, the best "date" she'd been on in a very long while. And it had been a long while, indeed. She and Stephen had parted ways over six months ago in the ugliest way imaginable. It had been a new low—even for her. But then the wedding plans kicked into high gear and the job from SoftWerx came through, leaving her with little time to think about anything else, much less men.

Just enjoy this for what it is.

As they sat finishing their wine, Matt asked her, "How did a girl from Alabama end up in Chicago? I thought Southerners were allergic to snow."

"We are." She laughed and swirled her wine in her glass. "First you have to understand something about kids who grow up in lower Alabama. Their entire teenage years are preoccupied with one thing—getting the hell out of Alabama. I wasn't any different. So when Northwestern offered me a track scholarship, I jumped on it and moved up here."

"That explains those amazing legs of yours."

Ella blushed at the unexpected compliment. *He thinks my legs are amazing.* She self-consciously uncrossed and recrossed her legs under the table. When she did, she accidentally slid one leg against his. He didn't move, so she simply enjoyed the pressure of his leg against hers as she sipped her wine.

"Are you fast?"

"What?" She choked on her wine and moved her leg away from his quickly, bumping the table hard as she did. Glassware rattled.

"On the track. Are you still fast?"

Oh, she thought, relieved. "I never was really fast. I ran cross-country. I'm a bit out of shape now, but I do still run for fun."

"Ah, stamina instead of speed. That's a good thing."

Was he flirting? That kind of put a new twist on the evening if he was. Her flirting skills were a bit rusty these days…

"Did you meet Melanie at Northwestern?"

The change in subject jarred a little, but she welcomed it. "We were roommates our freshman year. We lived together all through undergraduate school, then got an apartment together."

"You two are an unusual pair. You've got kind of a yin and yang thing going."

That caused her to laugh. "I've never heard it put quite that way before. But, yeah, we make a good team. Things were rough at the beginning, though. Melanie was out all night majoring in boys and beer, and I had to be up early for track practice. Unfortunately—or in our case, fortunately—University Housing didn't allow for room switching until a few weeks into the semester. By then we'd worked it out. I guess we've rubbed off a bit on each other over the years—filling in the holes, so to speak. It's going to be really tough to get used to not having her around all the time."

"Why move home now?" He relaxed back in his chair and casually draped an arm across the back of hers as he asked. The closeness of his body put hers on high alert, and she felt the fine hairs on the back of her neck rise to attention.

Just focus on the conversation. "Nine Chicago winters too many. Anyway, after spending all those years wanting to get out of Alabama, it didn't take all that long for me to realize how much I missed it. With Mel getting married and moving out anyway, the job offer seemed like fate or something. Moving while she's on her honeymoon keeps the goodbyes from being all weepy."

Matt offered her the last of the wine, and she held out her glass. Full of good food and enjoying both the view and the company, she wasn't in any hurry for dinner to end. He didn't seem in a rush, either, so she relaxed back in her chair, enjoying the slight weight of his arm against her.

"So what do you do with those degrees in computer science, Ella *Augustine* Mackenzie?"

The shock of hearing her middle name nearly caused her to choke on her wine again. Then she remembered pulling her degrees out from storage under the couch last week for packing and leaning them against the wall. He must have seen them earlier. "Hey, Augustine's a family name."

Matt snorted.

"What's *your* middle name, hotshot?"

"Matthew."

"Oh." *So much for that witty retort.* "What's your first name, then?"

"William." A smug smile twitched at the corners of his mouth.

"Lucky you. Well, William Matthew Jacobs, until two weeks ago, I was a software designer. Two weeks from now, I'll be the design team head at SoftWerx."

Matt let out an impressed whistle. "I've heard of them. Congratulations."

Pride bubbled up inside her. She'd been so caught up in the wedding, she hadn't had time to fully adjust to the idea of her success. "Your turn. How'd you end up in Atlanta?"

Matt sipped at his wine and signaled the server for the check. "Strictly business. I, too, went to college out of state—Ohio State, actually—but for different reasons than you. Did Melanie tell you I have five brothers?"

"Actually I've heard quite a bit about the Jacobs six-pack. I've even met a few."

"There you have it. I was tired of being 'that youngest Jacobs boy.' All five of my brothers stayed around here, so I had to be different and go out of state. I ended up at Penn for law school and got in with a local firm. They opened a new office in Atlanta two years later, and I was sent there." He shrugged as if his job was nothing—the law equivalent of flipping burgers at McDonald's. Something about the way he carried himself, though, made her think otherwise.

"What kind of law do you practice?"

"Mainly entertainment. I take care of a lot of the contracts for most of the major venues in town. A few local celebs keep us on retainer, as well."

"Anybody interesting?"

"Couldn't tell you even if I wanted to," he teased her.

"Do you like Atlanta? I haven't been there in years."

"I love it." His hand came to rest on Ella's shoulder. Rusty or not at the flirting thing, as his thumb slid lightly over her skin, even she could recognize he was flirting with her. She shivered at the sensation as all her blood seemed to rush to her skin. Focusing on the conversation took on a whole new level of difficulty. "All the excitement of Chicago without all the snow," he continued, and it took her a second to remember what they were talking about. "In fact, I've gotten a bit thin-blooded in the past few years, and I try to avoid coming up here at all in the winter."

She pulled herself together with a deep breath. "That must make coming home for Christmas a bit difficult."

"I don't think anyone notices when I don't make it."

"I don't believe *that* for a second."

"Seriously, we are the Catholic family cliché. You think Brian's family is bad? Mine's worse."

"I think Brian's family is nice—a little loud when they're all together, but…"

"Brian's got nothing on my family when it comes to loud. My mom and dad have nine brothers and sisters, so I have, let's see, um, twenty-two—no, twenty-*three*—first cousins. All my brothers are married and have two or three kids apiece. There's at least fifty people at my mom's house on any given holiday. *That* is the definition of loud."

She was such a sucker for the idea of a big family gathering—noisy or not. How could he be so blasé about it? "I'm sure they take note of who's there."

"Well, my brothers and I look a lot alike, so short of actually calling roll…" He sighed. "Do you have siblings?"

"No, it was just me and my grandparents."

"Consider yourself lucky. Everyone was at the house

today, and it was an absolute zoo. It's enough to drive a man crazy. I used to dream of being an only child. Sometimes I still do." Matt was the picture of the aggrieved youngest child, and Ella sipped at the last of her wine to stifle a laugh.

"And I used to dream about being in a big family. I mean, Mel's family has adopted me, for all intents and purposes, but it's not quite the same thing. I guess everyone wants what they don't have."

"Usually I'd say you were right. Especially after a day like today."

This time she did laugh. She couldn't help it. "Mel's told me about your mother. I can't imagine she's too happy with the lack of grandchildren from you."

"I hear it all the time. Someday I'll see what I can do about that. Right now it's not really an option."

Ella wondered about that statement as Matt moved away from her in order to pay. The light teasing tone that had marked their entire evening evaporated once they started talking about his family. Mel hadn't mentioned any rifts in the family—not beyond the norm, at least. Maybe he was just touchy about the whole get-married-and-have-kids thing. She could relate to that.

With Matt's arm gone, she missed the warmth that emanated from him. Although the restaurant temperature was comfortable, she shivered as the heat dissipated. Matt noticed.

"Do you need my jacket?" He was already lifting it off the back of his chair and holding it out to her.

"Your mama must have raised you right. Or else Southern manners have rubbed off on you."

"I will pass the compliment along to Mom." He continued to hold the jacket out to her.

"No, but thanks. I'm fine." She wrapped her shawl around her shoulders as Matt shrugged into his jacket.

But as they left the restaurant, the intimacy they shared also seemed to be left behind, because Matt didn't flirt with her at all on the way back to her apartment.

Even though it made the situation more complicated, she was more disappointed by that than she cared to admit.

CHAPTER THREE

THE frustration of shifting back to small talk after all that flirting had Ella balancing on her last nerve by the time they reached her apartment. Matt waited as she unlocked the door, then held it open as he ushered her in first.

"I'll just get those wedding presents out of the way for you." He followed her up the stairs.

"Thanks. Mel's brothers are coming Saturday to pick up her furniture and stuff to take to Brian's, but they didn't want to be responsible for moving the fragile things." She pointed in the direction of the boxes. "I'll go grab some tape to close them up so they'll be easier to carry. I'm going to change, too, if that's okay. I'll kill myself trying to carry stuff down the stairs in this getup." He nodded, and she added, "There's wine and beer in the fridge. Help yourself."

"Thanks. Can I get you anything?"

"Um, wine, please. The glasses are in the cupboard beside the microwave."

She could hear Matt opening and pouring the wine

as she rummaged for something to change into. Yoga pants and a baby tee were easiest to find in the rubble, but slightly revealing. She debated for a moment, but she couldn't bring herself to appear in front of a muffin like Matt in battered jeans or ratty sweats. Vanity won out over practicality, and she returned to the living room, twisting her hair up into a ponytail as she went.

When Matt's eyes widened appreciatively at her outfit, she had a momentary surge of girl power. He'd removed his jacket and rolled up his sleeves, and Ella hoped that meant he planned to stay for a little while. She really was enjoying his company, and the ego boost wasn't bad, either. He offered her one of the glasses with a smile.

"Thanks." She sipped at the Merlot before setting it aside, and kneeled on the floor next to some boxes to strap tape across their tops. In a conspiratorial tone she asked, "If I tell you something, will you promise not to tell Mel or Brian?"

Matt joined her on the floor. "Of course."

"I hate this china." She laughed. "Mel fell in love with it at first sight and registered for every piece they made. I didn't have the heart to tell her it was the ugliest thing I'd ever seen." She pulled out one of the overly colorful and flowery plates to show him. "What do you think?"

"Yikes. I can't believe Brian agreed to this." He took the plate from her hand, and his hand brushed hers. Again her senses jumped to red alert. Had the touch been accidental or intentional?

"As far as I know." She frowned in mock dismay. "It's

sad. Melanie has such good taste in everything else." He passed the ugly china back to her before leaning back against the couch and loosening his tie. *Another good sign he plans to stay for a while.*

"I promise your secret is safe with me. I just hope Mel never invites me to a fancy dinner party. I don't know if I can eat off that and keep it down."

Ella also leaned back against the couch. "Unless she calls in a caterer for the event, you have nothing to fear in that arena. I love her, but Mel is a lousy cook. About the only things she can make are scrambled eggs and peanut butter and jelly sandwiches. The last thing that girl needed was dishes."

"Uh-oh, better watch out. I may tell on you."

"That's an empty threat. God knows I've told her the same thing hundreds of times. I think one of the reasons she lived with me was because I could cook. I've tried to teach her over the years, but she's just a bit hopeless in the kitchen."

Matt tugged his tie the rest of the way off and placed it behind him on the couch. As he leaned forward, those chocolate eyes captured hers. "And you? What are you a bit hopeless at?"

Suddenly, the air felt thick, and her voice didn't seem to work very well. She cleared her throat and tried for a light, flirtatious tone. "A lady never admits her shortcomings."

"Come on. Tell me." His voice dropped, and Ella's temperature rose several degrees.

She swallowed hard around the knot in her throat. "That's a rather personal question, don't you think?"

He reached out to touch a lock of hair that had escaped her ponytail and trailed down the side of her face. Curling it around his finger, he said, "I don't think so. We all have small things we're just hopeless at. Me, I can't get my TiVo to stop taping *Brady Bunch* reruns. It's ridiculous."

The mood shifted the moment Matt touched her. Light flirtation was over. This was serious stuff. Ella tried to ignore his hand as he tucked the wayward strand behind her ear, but couldn't. He was stroking her earlobe, for heaven's sake. A shiver ran down her spine, and she couldn't stop herself from leaning, just slightly, into his hand.

"You, Ella, are beautiful, smart, and can single-handedly organize large weddings." He brushed her bangs back off her face. His hand slid down so that he cupped her cheek. His eyes locked with hers. "That's impressive."

He was so close Ella could feel his breath and the warmth radiating off his body. His voice and the gentleness of his hand hypnotized her. He had called her beautiful. This unbelievably gorgeous man had called *her* beautiful. Her mouth went dry, and she swallowed hard—again—but still couldn't get her voice above a whisper. "I'd say you were the impressive one."

To illustrate her point, she laid one hand on Matt's broad shoulder, slid it down to where his biceps bulged under his shirt and squeezed the hard muscle. She had meant to simply emphasize his size, but, at her touch, Matt's breath caught, and his hand reflexively curled around the nape of her neck to pull her closer to him.

"Glad to hear it," Matt whispered, and then his lips met hers. His first touch was gentle, almost hesitant, barely catching her bottom lip, but Ella leaned in to him. That small encouragement seemed to be all he needed, because his second kiss wasn't at all hesitant. His mouth moved over hers, forcefully seeking, and she put her arms around his neck. When her lips parted, Matt's tongue swept inside, sending bolts of pure desire to Ella's core.

She'd never felt anything like this before, the undiluted sensation of total lust that sent her senses spinning and chased all rational thought out of her head. All she knew was what she felt: the soft thickness of his hair as she held his head to keep him from moving away, the pressure of his body as he lowered her back onto the floor, the hardness of his body as he lay down next to her and pulled her firmly against him.

Bliss.

He was huge, solid muscle all over; she could feel the movement of the bunched muscles of his back and chest under her hands and the hard pressure of his thighs as his legs entwined with hers. His hands roamed restlessly down her back and over the curve of her hip as his lips moved across her jawline and down her neck to her shoulder. Heat rushed to each place his lips touched, causing her to shiver when his mouth moved away and air cooled the moisture left behind. As Matt's hand finally slid up to gently cup her breast, she gasped and arched into him.

It was the gasp that focused Matt's attention. His response to Ella amazed him and left him shaken. He'd wanted to taste her all evening, but he hadn't been prepared for the desire that had slammed through him the moment her tongue touched his. He hadn't been able to focus on anything but the feel of her since then. He wanted to touch her everywhere, all at once, and his hands slid across her body, learning her. But her gasp had snapped his attention back to Ella's face. It was his turn to catch his breath.

Ella's head was thrown back, her eyes closed. A flush spread across her cheeks, and she was breathing shallowly through her mouth. He now knew what lust looked like and was shocked by the same feeling rocketing through him. Carefully he squeezed the breast nestled in his hand, and he was rewarded when her teeth caught her lower lip in response.

She wasn't wearing a bra beneath her thin T-shirt, and her nipples were hard against the fabric. Caressing the soft curve of her, he leaned down to take her nipple between his lips, sucking her through the soft cotton. She arched again, this time more forcefully, as if electricity had shot through her. Her fingers tangled in his hair, holding him against her breast and encouraging him as the tip of his tongue flicked against the hard nub.

His hand came up to cover her other breast, kneading gently as he brought his thigh up between her legs to press against her.

Tugging on his head, Ella brought his mouth up to hers and kissed him as she moved restlessly against his thigh. Her tongue wrestled with his, and her hands pulled insistently at his shirt, tugging it out of the waistband of his slacks, and moving beneath to explore his skin.

The feel of her rocking against him was too arousing, and Matt slowly slid his thigh away from her. Something like a whimper escaped Ella at the loss, but was replaced with a sigh as his hand slid down to where his thigh had recently been. He could feel the heat of her through the thin pants she was wearing. With the heel of his hand, he pressed in hard, wringing a moan of pleasure from her lips.

The phone rang, jarring them both with the interruption.

Ella's eyes flew open, and he watched as the world came back into focus and reality forced the haze from her vision. Matt cursed and dropped his forehead to rest on hers. His own vision clearing, he met her gaze. Ella was stiff and still beneath him, and the location of his hand seemed wildly inappropriate all of a sudden. Her eyes were wide, filled with an emotion he couldn't identify. Whatever it was, it sure as hell wasn't passion.

Another loud ring, and he whispered, "Ignore it." He heard the machine pick up, then Melanie's voice filled the room.

"El? It's me. Pick up if you're there." Even he could hear the tears in her voice. Something was wrong.

The sound of Melanie's tears galvanized Ella into action. Scrambling, she managed to slide out from under him, and hurried across the room to grab the phone. "Mel, I'm here. What's wrong? Is everything okay?"

Ella had her back to him, but when her shoulders dropped with relief, he knew that whatever had Melanie calling home from her honeymoon in tears couldn't be too disastrous. He sat up and dragged a hand through his hair, feeling the spikes created by Ella's hands. Uncomfortable, he adjusted himself, and with a deep shuddering breath, he tried to bring his overheated body under control. Grabbing his glass of wine from earlier, he drank deeply and tried to decipher what was going on from only one side of a conversation.

"Yeah, I'm fine... Mel, what's wrong?... Because you're on your honeymoon... Well, where's Brian?... Are you sure everything's okay?... Are you drunk?" A long pause. "I'm going to miss you, too, but... You're on your honeymoon. Mel? Calm down, sweetie. Mel? Melanie! Fine. Look, let me talk to Brian." Another long pause. "Brian! What's going on?... Okay... Uh-huh... Well, don't let her do that. You're on your honeymoon, for God's sake. Go out, have fun, have sex or something, and just tell her to call me once she gets back home... Uh-huh... All right, then, talk to you later."

Ella hung up the phone, but she didn't turn around. He could tell by the way she squared her shoulders that she wouldn't be coming back to where they'd left off. His body protested the thought, every nerve screaming for him to drag her back under him. He hadn't been this worked up with no release in sight since high school.

The next time Melanie hit him up for concert tickets, he would take great pleasure in turning her down.

With the phone in its cradle, Ella knew she'd have to turn and face Matt. *Keep it light. Don't make yourself look dumb.*

She slapped a smile on her face and turned. With a small shrug, she explained the odd phone call. "Mel really shouldn't drink. She gets all maudlin and weepy. Brian left the room to get ice, and she calls me to tell me how much she's going to miss not living with me." She tried a small laugh, but it was a bit forced sounding and she knew it. "Brian was kind of shocked when he returned and found her weeping on the telephone…" She couldn't meet Matt's eyes, and her words trailed off into uncomfortable silence. Belatedly she realized her very disheveled state and began adjusting her clothes and pushing her hair back into its ponytail.

She had to be insane, making out with Matt like she was some hormone-crazed teenager. She barely knew him, yet if the phone hadn't rung when it did, she knew she'd be naked and in bed with him by now. Even if it would be a mistake to sleep with one of Brian's friends, the thought wasn't an unpleasant one. In fact, the thought was more than a bit tempting.

She had to be crazy to even consider it.

Somehow, though, she just couldn't bring herself to feel as crazy as she thought she should. In her entire life, she'd never had an honest-to-goodness, no-strings-attached, one-night stand, but Matt definitely would have been a grand choice for a first time—even with the possible repercussions.

It had been a bad idea, and she should thank Melanie for her unwitting save. She'd be better off in the long run without this complication.

The silence was deafening and growing longer and more uncomfortable by the minute as the easiness they'd enjoyed all evening evaporated. Ella wasn't sure how to get it back—and she wasn't even sure if she should try, all things considered—but she needed to say *something*. But what?

Matt cleared his throat, breaking the silence, and Ella jumped. "Ella, I, um…" He paused, and she finally got the nerve up to look at him. He was as disheveled as she, his shirt half-unbuttoned and untucked where she had been desperate to touch his skin, his hair rumpled from her hands. She noticed him staring at her chest. Looking down, she saw the damp spot where his mouth had closed over her nipple, and she hurriedly crossed her arms across her breasts.

He cleared his throat again, as if speaking was difficult. "I guess I should go. I'll just, um, call you tomorrow, and come by and pick up those presents."

"Okay." What on earth was she supposed to say? He

seemed as uncomfortable as she was, but his willingness to bolt for the door was slightly offensive to her ego. As she walked down the stairs to show him out, she found herself cursing Melanie's bad timing. Earlier she had been caught up in the moment, spontaneously taking advantage of the situation. Now she actually had to think about what she was doing, and she was tired of always thinking rather than doing. The whole situation was frustrating as hell.

Hand on the doorknob, Matt paused and turned to her. She stood on the second step, making her eye level with him for the first, nonhorizontal time. "You were great tonight."

"Excuse me?"

He hurried ahead. "At dinner, I mean. Not that you weren't great under—I mean *after*—um. Damn." He took a deep breath. "I'm really making a mess of this. What I mean is that I had a great time tonight."

Somehow his discomfiture alleviated a bit of her own. "Me, too." She smiled, a genuine one this time.

"Good night." He leaned in to kiss her, and Ella met him halfway, expecting a quick, perfunctory kiss. Instead he kissed her long and hard—not with the all-consuming passion she had felt earlier, but still filled with a longing that was unbelievably erotic. She kissed him back, and he lifted her off her feet, crushing her against him.

Minutes—or possibly hours, she had no sense of anything when Matt kissed her—later, her back against the wall of the entryway, Matt finally broke the kiss and lowered her onto her feet. Thankfully, he didn't let her go, because her legs were too shaky from the kiss to hold her upright. He held her loosely and rested his chin on top of her head.

"Wow." He took a deep breath and released it noisily. "Okay, I'm going to go now. I really don't want to, but I should."

From her position, head nestled in his chest, she could feel his heart pounding against her cheek, and there was no mistaking the feel of his erection pressing into her. She knew that those weren't just polite, empty words.

"Then don't."

CHAPTER FOUR

SHE said the words quietly, but Matt tensed as if she had shouted at him.

He pulled back to look down at her, surprise written across his face. "What?"

"If you don't want to leave, you don't have to. I'd like it if you stayed." Ella couldn't believe the words she heard coming out of her own mouth, but she was sure she meant them. She liked Matt; she enjoyed talking to him and spending time with him. And, if their earlier foreplay was any indication, he was practically guaranteed to be fabulous in bed. She was leaving Chicago and this chapter of her life behind her, so consequences be damned. This time next week she'd be back home and starting a new life. She was absolutely free to do anything she wanted, and she wanted to do Matt Jacobs. She placed her hand on his cheek and smiled. "Really."

Matt didn't ask her again. He swept her up into his arms and bounded up the stairs two at a time, carrying her as if she didn't weigh anything at all. He deftly dodged the boxes in the living room and headed directly for Ella's bedroom. Her bedside lamp was still on from her quick change earlier that evening, and he was able to wind his way through the chaos without any problems, laying her gently in the middle of her bed.

Ella knew she fit the technical definition of petite, but no one had ever made her feel as tiny and delicate as Matt. He practically loomed over her as he removed the jacket he had put back on earlier. In the semidarkness of her room, she felt like the heroine of some romance novel—the virgin princess about to be ravished by the Viking lord—and she was very much looking forward to it.

His shirt was still untucked and partially unbuttoned from their earlier play, and he stood beside the bed watching her as he slid the final few buttons out of their holes and shrugged out of it. Her mouth watered at the seeming acres of tanned skin and hard muscle he offered. Seeing him reach for the waistband of his pants, she sat up, grabbed the hem of her T-shirt, and started shimmying it up her body.

"Don't."

"What?" Ella was confused by the remark, but she stilled nonetheless.

"I want to undress you myself."

Maybe it was the statement, or maybe it was the huskiness of his voice, but hands down it was the most erotic statement she'd ever heard. Her body agreed; she could feel her nipples hardening again and an ache building between her legs. With a casualness she didn't actually feel, she leaned back against the pillows, waiting for him to finish undressing and join her.

But, *oh,* what a sight he treated her to. A fully dressed Matt was unbelievably handsome. Nude, he was simply jaw-dropping. Six-pack abs, narrow waist, well-defined legs—her hands itched to trace the lines of those muscles. She wished she were a sculptor; the man had a body that needed to be immortalized in clay.

Just the sight of him caused all the moisture to drain from her mouth and go rushing south. When she realized she was staring openmouthed at him, she forced her eyes back to his face, hoping he hadn't noticed.

If he had, he was gallant enough not to mention it as he joined her on the bed. Instead he kissed her, slowly and thoroughly, as though he was memorizing the feel of her mouth. His hands meandered over her body with torturous slowness, driving her insane with wanting. She wanted to touch him all over, learn the taste of his skin, investigate that six-pack with her tongue. Finally he slid her T-shirt up and over her head and she had the skin-to-skin contact she craved. His hard pecs flattened her breasts, and she could feel the slight tickle of crisp hair against her nipples. She only got to savor the feeling for a moment as he kissed her deeply and more urgently than earlier, before he rolled her onto her back and began a leisurely exploration of her breasts and belly.

She hissed with pleasure when his tongue snaked out to taste her nipple, teasing it to an aching point. She tugged at his hair, wanting more, and moaned when he finally pulled her nipple into the wet heat of his mouth. Fire licked through her as her hips echoed the tug of his lips. She wanted more—all of him, *now*—but Matt was in no hurry as he moved that amazing mouth to her other breast.

She writhed beneath him as he finally licked and kissed and nibbled his way down her ribs to her navel and the waistband of her pants. Slowly, his tongue tasting each inch of skin as he exposed it, he inched her pants and panties down over her hips. Sitting up, he finally slid them the rest of the way down her legs, leaving her naked. He stared at her, his eyes moving from the top of her head to the tips of her toes, until she began to squirm uncomfortably beneath the scrutiny.

"You're so beautiful. Every inch of you is perfect." Something low in her belly flopped over at his words, but she couldn't stop to question it.

His hand slid slowly up her leg from ankle to calf where he gently squeezed the muscle before moving his head down to kiss her knee. Ella could barely breathe as he placed soft, sucking kisses on her inner thighs, moving slowly higher until his breath was tickling her dark pubic curls. He nuzzled her briefly, teasing her, before sliding his tongue in to taste her.

A short, strangled cry of pleasure escaped her, and she couldn't stop herself from lifting her hips to his mouth and threading her hands though his hair to hold him there. Understanding, Matt slid his arms under and around her thighs, holding her in place while his tongue moved over her heated flesh before pushing up into her. She bucked in response, but released her hold on his head to reach behind her to grab the headboard for support. Her head thrashed back and forth as she approached her climax, and when she reached it, she screamed Matt's name.

The trembling in her legs still hadn't stopped as Matt pushed himself up and over her, kissing her hard. She could taste herself on his lips, and his erection throbbed insistently against her belly.

"Condoms?" he whispered.

Ella had lost the ability to understand English. "Huh?"

"Condoms. I didn't come prepared for this." He moved restlessly against her. "Please tell me you have some."

"Oh." Understanding pushed through the haze in her brain. She rolled over to the bedside table and rummaged through the rubble inside. *Dammit, where were they?* She knew they were in there somewhere, but Matt's hand stroking down her spine to caress her backside was too distracting for her to function properly.

She forgot what she was doing when he slid one strong finger inside her from behind. She shivered as he withdrew. *What was she looking for again?* As he slid another finger inside, her hips bucked, and she remembered. Trying to hold the thought against the wave of lust building, she groped in the drawer. Finally her hand closed over a foil packet, and she rolled back to him, triumphant.

"Thank heaven," he sighed, tearing into it. The relief in his voice would have been funny if she wasn't in such desperate physical need. He was fast and efficient, and in no time he was pulling her close. With another deep, drugging kiss, he nudged her knees apart and positioned himself between her thighs.

Wrapping her legs around his waist, Ella wasted no time as she pulled his head down for another kiss and raised her hips to meet his. Matt slid into her with agonizing slowness and caught her gasp of pleasure with his mouth.

Oh. Dear. Heaven. Heat licked at her insides as he withdrew, repositioned her hips, and pushed home. Those powerful biceps trembled as he braced himself on his arms and set a leisurely pace she was sure would kill her with anticipation.

Ella met each thrust as she returned to the peak she'd only just descended. Greedy for more, she gripped his hips, her fingernails biting into his skin as she tried to increase his tempo. It was so good—she should slow down and try to prolong the pleasure. But it was too good to slow down.

Long, lovely shivers moved through her with each thrust, pushing her closer to the edge as sanity spun away. Her universe centered on the hardness filling her as stars exploded behind her eyelids. She reached her climax for the second time, going over the precipice just as Matt gave one last, deep thrust and collapsed on top of her with a groan.

She was panting and slick with sweat, but as she floated back down, she realized so was he. Unwilling to move too much, she slid her hands over the damp planes of his back and neck as the afterglow hummed through her.

Matt took several deep, gulping breaths before he pushed himself up on his elbows and looked down at her. For a moment she was simply lost in those chocolate eyes as her heartbeat slowed and her breathing returned to normal.

Matt finally broke that intimate stare by leaning down to kiss her. With a rueful grin he placed his forehead on hers. "Sorry. That was a bit faster than I intended."

"I'm not complaining." *In fact I'm thanking my lucky stars.* She unclamped her legs from his waist, stretching them languorously before relaxing. Another small shudder ran through her, and goose bumps rose across sweat-cooled skin. "I don't think I could've waited much longer."

Matt rolled off her and then grabbed the sheet from the foot of the bed to pull up over them both. He lightly pushed the hair back from her face. "You are amazing." He stole one last quick kiss before sliding out of the bed with an "I'll be right back" and padding for her bathroom. "I won't be in so much of a hurry next time," he promised as he disappeared around the corner.

"Next time?" Ella rolled onto her side, facing the bathroom.

"Of course." Matt came back into the room to sit on the side of her bed. Running his hand along her sheet-covered thigh, he attempted a leer. "That was only the beginning of what I plan to do with you." Opening the drawer he'd seen her rummage through earlier, he searched for, and found, more condoms. Pulling the strip out of the drawer, he let it trail across the bed meaningfully.

"You, my dear, are in for a long night."

Ella woke to sunlight streaming across the bed. It took her a minute to realize she was alone in the bed and another to figure out why she had the unusual feeling she shouldn't be.

Matt.

Sitting up, she listened carefully, but no sounds of life came from the rest of the apartment. "Matt?" she called. No answer. She ran her hand along the side of the bed where he had slept. It was cold. He'd obviously been gone for a long time.

With a sigh Ella flopped back onto the pillow. Why did she have a little niggle of disappointment because he left without saying goodbye? Hell, she should be wondering why she let him spend the night in the first place. She *never* allowed sleepovers. Actually *sleeping* with someone was an intimacy she only rarely participated in, and certainly not in her bed.

Then why hadn't she shown him the door in the wee hours of the morning? Her disappointment at his disappearance bothered her. It was better this way—she could avoid all the uncomfortable morning-after small talk—but still…being proven right again brought little satisfaction.

Stretching under the covers, she felt a slight soreness. Well, *that* was understandable, considering the sexual gymnastics she'd participated in. Matt certainly had stamina. And imagination. And the ability to please.

Oh, *mercy,* he had the ability to please, all right. And then some.

She didn't really remember when or how it had all ended, but it had certainly been fun while it lasted.

But it was over. *Now back to my regularly scheduled life.* As she glanced around the room, the monumental job of packing stared back at her, reminding her what she had to do. It was enough to make her want to crawl back under the duvet. She considered it seriously before she tossed back the covers with a groan and forced herself out of the bed.

She grabbed a T-shirt off the floor and pulled it over her head for the short walk to the kitchen to get a cola out of the fridge. Caffeine and sugar—that's what she needed to get her moving.

As the cola worked its magic on her sluggish body, she ran a hand through the tangle of her hair and grimaced. What she really needed was a hot shower. She sniffed. Matt's scent clung to her skin like afterglow. She absolutely reeked of sex.

In the shower she let the hot water massage the soreness from her muscles as she replayed in her head bits and pieces of the night before.

She should be blushing at the memories of the way she'd gone at Matt and the things they'd done, but as she pulled back the shower curtain, she caught a glimpse of herself in the mirror. That wasn't a blush—that was a self-satisfied smirk.

Humming, she dried her hair and slid into a pair of battered jeans and her favorite Cubs T-shirt. Okay, so she'd broken half a dozen of her own rules—with her best friend's husband's best friend, no less—but she was still in an unbelievably good mood.

There was definitely something liberating in doing something completely out of character. She felt like a new woman—a night with Matt had been exactly what she needed.

Still humming and unable to wipe that smirk off her face, she returned to her bedroom.

"Good morning."

Ella screamed, her hand flying to her throat in shock as she turned to find the voice. Matt was sitting on the bed.

"Matt! Good Lord, you scared the life out of me!" Heart pounding, she leaned against her dresser. "I didn't know you were here."

What was he doing here?

"Sorry, I didn't mean to scare you. You were sleeping pretty soundly, and I'd hoped to get back before you woke up." He indicated a box from a local bakery sitting squarely in the middle of her bed. "I brought breakfast."

She still hadn't moved, so he came to stand in front of her. He ran his hands up her arms. "Boy, I really did give you a bit of a shock. I was going to fix something and serve it to you in bed, but the cupboard was bare.

You know, for a girl who claims to know how to cook, there's a shocking lack of food in your kitchen."

"Yeah, well, I haven't had much time to grocery shop recently," she answered absently. Her pulse was returning to normal, but she was still having problems forming coherent thoughts. He went to get breakfast?

"Come on." He led her to the bed. "I ran over to Brian's to grab some clothes and hit the bakery on the way back. I did leave you a note by the way—in the kitchen."

"I didn't see it. Sorry." She hadn't even thought to look for a note. But the comment about clothes caught her attention, and she realized that the khakis and shirt were gone, and he was as casually dressed as she, in snug, faded jeans and a gray T-shirt. He looked more like a fraternity rat than a high-flying lawyer. His damp hair and freshly shaved face made her very glad she'd headed to the shower first thing this morning.

Matt presented the bakery box to her and pulled the top back with a flourish. "I wasn't sure what you liked, so I got a bit of everything. Bagels, croissants, Danishes, take your pick. I've also got coffee, tea and orange juice."

What to say? "Um, thanks. It all looks great." She picked a bagel loaded with cream cheese out of the box and nibbled on it absently. He was certainly in a good mood. Matt leaned back on the pillows and grabbed the other bagel out of the box. He continued to chatter on, completely at ease, while she struggled to get her scattered thoughts in some semblance of order.

It wasn't working.

"Ella?"

She looked up to find him holding out a cup to her. "Huh?"

"I asked if you wanted the coffee." He looked at her closely. "Are you okay? You seem a little out of it."

You think? "I'm fine. Really. I'm just not much of a morning person." That excuse seemed much better than the truth—the truth being that she didn't have a single clue what she should be saying right now. "The tea, please. That'll help." Ella reached for the other steaming cup and tried to find a light tone. "Is there milk?"

Matt continued to study her face as he handed her both cream and sugar. Ella found it very disconcerting, but she tried not to look uncomfortable. She flashed him another, but bigger, smile and took a bite of her bagel. "They have the best bagels in Chicago, you know. Some folks think that place downtown under the El track is better, but I like theirs…" She trailed off, unable to keep babbling aimlessly under Matt's intense scrutiny.

"Oh, I get it now." Matt nodded in realization. "You thought I'd left, didn't you?"

Ella started to shake her head in denial, but he continued on. "That's why you were so startled to see me. You thought I'd just snuck out of here in the middle of the night."

Defeated at her attempts to even act at ease, Ella admitted it. "All right. Yes, I thought you were gone, so I was a bit surprised to find you here."

Reaching out to stroke her arm lightly, Matt smiled. "After last night? Not a chance."

A warm glow settled in her belly. She tried to ignore it.

Pausing, his smile faded and he pulled his hand away. "Unless, of course, you were glad I wasn't here. Did you want me to just leave? I mean, if you don't want…" He started to stand up.

The mattress moved as he did, sending them both scrambling to catch the cups before they dumped their contents onto the bed. Somehow, the sight of Matt juggling cups of juice and coffee while still holding a half-eaten bagel worked wonders at alleviating much of Ella's unease. She laughed, some of the previous night's closeness returning.

"No. Sit. Carefully," she added as he continued his juggling act. "I'm glad you're here." As surprising as it seemed, she meant it. "I'm just a bit new at this."

"What 'this' are you new at?" he asked, placing everything on more stable surfaces and returning to the bed.

"This." She circled her hands to include him, her and the bed. "You, me, breakfast." Flustered, she threw her hands up in defeat and looked at him levelly. She settled on the plain truth. "To be completely honest, I don't usually do sleepovers. And certainly not here. I'm not quite sure of the morning-after etiquette."

"The etiquette?" A laugh escaped, and Ella narrowed her eyes at him as he tried to cover it with a cough. "I'm hardly an expert, but I've never really thought of it that way before. But, by all means, we should follow proper etiquette." He leaned back against the headboard in mock seriousness. "You're Southern, so you know the importance of thank-you notes." He grinned as he easily ducked the bagel she tossed at him. "And then there's the giving of expensive gifts—the value, of course, should be dependent on how good the sex was." Ella looked for something bigger to throw at him. Matt waggled his eyebrows at her suggestively as he continued. "Oh, and we can't forget the traditional farewell blow j— Oorph." He was cut off as Ella lunged at him and landed squarely on his chest.

"You are evil, Matt Jacobs. Don't you dare make fun of me."

The laughter faded from his voice. "I wouldn't dream of it." He wrapped his arms around her and rolled her onto her side. His face, only inches from hers, blocked out everything else, and Ella found herself trapped by those chocolate-colored eyes again. "Seriously, though, if you want me to leave, just say so and I will." When she shook her head, he kissed her lightly. "Good, 'cause I've been thinking."

There was that glowy feeling again. "Really. Is that what you call it?"

"Hush." He slid one hand up and down her side. "Those legs of yours are distracting enough to my thought process." Ella could have argued that his hands were actually more distracting. She just wasn't able to think properly while in close proximity to him. "What I'd really like to do is take you back to bed and keep you naked for the next few days while we explore every position in the *Kama Sutra*. But I also know that you have a moving truck coming on Friday and a ton of packing left to do."

Her mind reeled at the thought of days of naked decadence, but she managed a nod. Not that she cared about the moving truck right now.

"I'm in town until Saturday. I'm willing to help you pack—in between my attempts to drag you back in here, of course."

Huh? "But don't you have plans already made for this week?"

He sighed. "Well, I had originally planned to spend some time with my family, but I got *that* out of my system yesterday."

"You are terrible. I'm sure your mother expects to see more of you than that."

"Probably. But too much family togetherness isn't good." She started to interrupt, but he shook his head. "Seriously. I love my family and all, but they drive me completely insane. In fact—" he paused and looked the tiniest bit chagrined "—they think that my flight leaves today."

"You should be ashamed of yourself."

"Oh, I am. Trust me." His hands stopped their aimless wandering and became much more specific in their target, sliding under the waistband of her jeans to caress the base of her spine. She shivered. "Deeply, deeply ashamed."

As he pulled her in closer, Matt's lips met hers for a

long, hot kiss. His hips pressed against her, and she could feel the hardness of his erection through the fabric that separated them. Aroused again, she returned his kiss with all the heat inside of her. Reaching a hand between them, she stroked the hard bulge straining against his zipper.

Groaning, he pushed against her hand, and Ella tugged at the snap and zipper, freeing him, then sliding her hand up and down the warm smoothness of him. Matt's breath caught, and he moved against her hand urgently, his tongue sliding against hers in an erotic promise of things to come.

She slid down his body to replace her hand with her mouth. Matt's back arched as he helped tug his jeans over his hips and out of her way. His hands came down to tangle in her hair as she ran her tongue around the throbbing head and sucked him hard.

She heard his short, sharp intake of breath, followed by a husky whisper. "Ella."

His hips moved, causing him to slide, ever so slightly, in and out of her mouth as her hand slid around to gently cup his balls. He bucked in response and she tasted saltiness on the very tip of him before he grabbed her head to pull her away.

"You're too good at that."

Catching her under the shoulders, he dragged her up for a ravaging kiss, his hands working furiously on her clothes and his. His kiss was mind scrambling, and Ella was clumsy at her attempts to help, tangling her legs in her jeans before kicking them away. How Matt got his jeans off, she didn't know, but she could feel the crisp hair of his legs tickling against hers as his fingers sought her with unerring accuracy. The first featherlight touch had her arching into his hand, begging for more. With a twist of his hand, he pressed two fingers up into her, matching the in and out rhythm of his fingers to the circling of his thumb.

Too much. She opened her eyes to tell him, only to find him watching her face. "That's it. Let go." As his talented fingers quickened their pace, she had no choice.

Finally, over the blood pounding in her ears and the gasps she dimly realized were coming from her, she heard the beautiful sound of him ripping into a foil packet.

Seconds later he pushed into her in one smooth, powerful stroke, embedding himself firmly in her wet warmth. Ella only had a brief moment to savor the feeling of fullness before he began moving, thrusting into her, absorbing her sharp cries of pleasure into his mouth. This was no long, leisurely replay of the night before. It was bald aching need bordering on pure lust, as if they'd never touched before.

The sharp edge should have been dulled last night, but to her surprise it was as keen and driving as the first time.

Ella's mind went blank, and she gave in to the need gripping her, her hips rising to meet each thrust, her arms wrapped tightly around his shoulders as she held on to him. She climaxed again with a hoarse scream, and

Matt redoubled his efforts, pounding deeply into her—once, twice, three times more—before stiffening as he reached his own orgasm.

Reality was slow to return, but as it did, she realized she was covered almost completely by Matt's body. She couldn't move even if she wanted to. She was doing well to breathe—not that breathing meant much to her, either. Matt's weight pressed her into the softness of the bed, and her head was buried in his shoulder. Which—she just realized—was still covered in gray cotton. With a giggle, she realized that she was still in her T-shirt as well.

"What's so funny?" Matt's voice was muffled by her hair, and he still sounded a bit out of breath.

"I thought you said you wanted to get naked."

Matt lifted his head to look at her. Puzzlement played across his face until she pointedly plucked at the fabric stretched across his shoulders.

"Well, hopefully there's still time for that." Moving just slightly in her, he coaxed, "So what do you say?"

She couldn't think properly. "To what?"

"To us spending this week together."

"But what about your family?" Ella couldn't let him ignore familial obligations.

He sighed. "How about if I promise to come home for the holidays—Thanksgiving *and* Christmas. I'll do the whole family thing then, okay?"

It was an awkward situation, and growing more so each second. And considering the position she was in… "And you'll help me pack?"

"Of course."

"Then what happens?" She looked at him levelly.

"What do you mean?" Matt rolled off her and sat up, and she did the same. She felt oddly exposed, considering what they'd just done, so she pulled the sheet up over herself in belated modesty.

She brushed her hair back out of her face and took a deep breath, determined to say what she needed to say without getting too flustered. "I'm not sure that's a good idea. The obvious benefits aside, of course," she added at his disbelieving look. "I like you, Matt, and last night—and everything else—was great. But it could be a really bad idea for us to go any further. My best friend is married to your best friend. This could all get very messy. And I don't want that."

Matt looked deliciously rumpled, and that distracted her as he pulled his hands through his hair in exasperation. "My life is crazy, Ella. I work sixty hours a week, and this is the first vacation I've had in years. I'd like to spend it with you. No games. No messiness. Just this week before you go on with your life and I go back to mine."

Any other woman might have found such an offer insulting, and Ella wondered how he possibly knew she wouldn't be. No-strings sex. For a week. With Matt. Her body was already on board, but the rational part of her brain not controlled by her libido was sending up multiple reasons why she should say no. If she were smart, she'd listen.

But she never claimed to be smart.

She had to admire his honesty and the way he simply spelled out what he wanted. And he was right, she told herself, it didn't have to get messy. Every decision in life didn't have to be analyzed to death first. Everything didn't have to be of earth-shattering importance.

A fling. He was offering her a fling. A wicked little shiver went through her as she realized she was going to do it. *Yay!* a little voice inside her crowed, drowning out the other little voice screaming in shock from her decision.

"You know, you're right. It doesn't have to get messy." The look on Matt's face was comic—part shock, part disbelief, part excitement. "What's wrong? You wanted me to say no?"

"No! I wanted you to say yes, I just—I guess—I expected you to say no. Possibly even slap my face and kick me out of here." His voice dropped to a growl. "But I'm very glad you said yes." He slid down on the pillows and pulled Ella on top to straddle him, obviously intent on starting right away.

Instead she slid off him and stood up beside the bed. Catching her hand, Matt tried to pull her back to him.

"Nope." She shook her head. Grabbing his pants off the floor, she tossed them to him before retrieving her own and putting them on. When he just lay there, she ordered, "Come on, now. Get dressed."

"El-*la*," he moaned and reached for her again.

"You promised me packing. I want to be sure I'm getting my end of this bargain." With a groan, Matt pulled the pillow over his head. She slapped him playfully on the leg. "Let's go. Manual labor time. Let's put those muscles to work."

She grabbed her now-cold cup of tea off the floor and headed for the kitchen to warm it up. Pausing, she turned back to the bed. Matt hadn't moved.

"Get up. Maybe later we'll play Handsome Moving Man and the Lonely Single Woman."

He peeked out from under the pillow. "Promise?"

"Depends on how much work you get done." Laughing, she ran for the door as Matt lunged for her.

CHAPTER FIVE

"'You are imaginative and innovative.' Well, that's good to know." Ella tossed the paper fortune from her cookie on the table and grinned at him.

"In bed," Matt added automatically. "And I'd agree."

Ella laughed and picked up her take-out box. She leaned back in her chair as she ate, and he watched her maneuver the chopsticks with ease. The sun setting behind the building next door left the room in half-light and created an intimate atmosphere.

With her hair pulled back into a ponytail, no makeup and wearing nothing but a shirt three sizes too big for her, she looked barely old enough to drive. In fact, she looked like every teenage boy's wet dream. Hell, she was certainly *his* wet dream come true. He remembered all the times Melanie or Brian had mentioned her in passing, and he'd never given her a second thought. He should have come home for a visit years ago....

When she looked up and found him staring at her, a half smile pulled at the corner of her mouth. "What now?"

"Why aren't you married, Ella?"

Ella's eyes widened in shock, and she coughed as lo mein noodles went down the wrong way. *Maybe I should've eased into that question. Or at least waited until her mouth wasn't full.* He waited as she caught her breath.

"Excuse me?"

"I'm just wondering why you're not married yet."

"I could ask you the same question," she said.

"Ah, but I asked you first." In the past few days, he felt he'd gotten to know Ella pretty well. Other than quick forays out for necessities like food and condoms, he'd spent every second with this woman. And, for once, constant togetherness wasn't fraying his nerves.

Maybe it was the nature of the situation, but unlike any other woman he'd ever spent time with, Matt felt he could say anything to Ella. Whether it was political debate or the eclectic nature of her CD collection, he hadn't had the need to self-censor or think twice about what he wanted to say. The rather abrupt nature of his question was the result. But it was out there now, and he wanted to know the answer.

Ella toyed with her food. "That's an impossible question to answer. Too many variables."

"Quit dodging my question. Do you want to get married?"

At that Ella grinned at him cheekily. "Is that a proposal?"

It was his turn to choke on Chinese food. "Hardly. Just a request for information."

"Maybe the right guy hasn't asked me yet."

"That's a cop-out. Try again."

"How about 'I haven't found anyone I'd want to spend the rest of my life with.' Will that satisfy your nosiness?"

He nodded in mock understanding. "I see. Commitment issues. Ow!" he added as she kicked him under the table.

"Oh, you're one to talk about commitment issues." She leaned back in her chair again and pointed chopsticks at him as she talked. "Let's look at your dating history, shall we? From what I've heard, you're not exactly a serial monogamist."

She had him there. Obviously, Melanie had a big mouth and no problem sharing details. "But there's a difference. I fully *intend* to meet a nice girl and settle down one day. My mother expects more grandchildren, you know. I should be a full partner by the time I'm thirty-five, and then I'll have time to be a family man. What's your excuse?"

Ella just shrugged and stared into her noodles. He waited and let the silence stretch out. Finally she stabbed her chopsticks into the noodles and placed the carton on the table.

She rolled her eyes to the ceiling. "I can't believe I'm even considering having this conversation with you."

"Why not?"

She took a deep breath and let it out noisily. "Melanie calls it 'emotional abstinence.' For me, relationships are a good idea in theory, but the practice trips me up every time. Call it what you like, but let's just say I haven't felt like I could make a guarantee to anyone."

"Life doesn't come with guarantees. You just do the best you can."

"And just hope for the best? That's not my style."

"You really are a control freak, aren't you?"

"Pretty much." She shrugged. "It's worked for me so far."

"If that's what you think—"

Suddenly Ella perked up and smiled at him. "You know, maybe I should be looking to get married. Weddings are fun." She was in his lap in two quick steps, her thighs straddling his hips. She took his box of noodles from his hand and slid it away, then settled against him suggestively. "I've found that you meet the most *interesting* people at weddings."

Her hands skimmed over his shoulders as she spoke, and his blood stirred. His mind might see her distraction ploy as clear as day, but his body didn't care. If there was a limit on how much sex a man could have every day and still function, he had to be close to it. But that didn't seem to stop all the blood in his body from rushing to his lap with the least encouragement. All Ella had to do was *breathe* in his general direction, and he was raring to go.

Her tongue snaked out to tease the skin beneath his ear, and a hot shiver ran through him. He surged to his feet, and Ella locked her ankles around his waist as he covered the short distance to her bedroom.

The contents of Ella's closet covered most of her bed and he randomly pushed suits and shoes aside in search of a space large enough to get her horizontal. Thankfully she was tiny; three swipes with his arm was all it took to clear a small patch of sheets. Ella clung to him like a tree frog as he knelt on the edge of the bed.

But his knee landed on something slippery, throwing him off balance and sending them both crashing to the floor. His head hit something hard, and stars exploded behind his eyelids.

"Ow. Damn."

"Oh, are you okay?" Ella fought with the coat slithering off the bed on top of them—the slippery fabric of the lining must've caused the fall—and attempted to keep the rest of the pile from avalanching off the bed.

He sat up, rubbing the lump forming on the back of his head. "Just minorly concussed. Anyone ever tell you that you own too much stuff?"

Ella grabbed the snow boots digging into his back and raised her eyebrows at him. "Do you need ice?"

He started to shake his head, but winced at the pain caused by the movement. "I'm fine. What did I hit?"

"No telling."

The cause of his pain was easy enough to find: a stack of unframed canvases partially hidden under a pile of T-shirts. "Here we are."

"Matt, wait—"

He pulled the top one off the stack and turned it over.

It was a watercolor of the Buckingham Fountain, the lights and jets of the evening show caught in an Impressionist style.

"That's, um… It's…" Ella's stammers drifted off to silence, and she wouldn't meet his eyes.

"You're blushing, El. I didn't think you could."

Ella chewed her lip, obviously embarrassed.

The artist's initials were in the bottom right corner. E.A.M. Ella Augustine Mackenzie. "Did you paint these?"

She blushed an even deeper shade of pink. "It's kind of a hobby." She reached for the canvas he held and moved protectively in front of the stack.

Being bigger than her had its advantages. It was easy enough to dodge her and retrieve the other paintings. He wasn't an expert in art, but he knew enough to see Ella had plenty of talent. The Chicago skyline. Lake Michigan. A cottage on a white sandy beach. Each one echoed a different style—from the classics to modern—but together they had a unifying feeling. A few minutes of close study while Ella fidgeted uncomfortably and he saw it: the attention to the play of light and the patterns it created. "You paint the light."

She nodded. "You surprise me, Matt. I didn't know you were into art."

"I'm not an expert, but I did take classes in college and my firm is a major patron in Atlanta. I've learned quite a bit, so I can honestly say these are good."

"Thanks." She relaxed at the compliment and nodded at the beachscape he still held. "That's home."

"It's beautiful," he said and was rewarded with a small, self-conscious smile. "I mean it, El. *Really* good. Do you sell any?"

She laughed and restacked the canvases. "Lord, no. I paint to relax and because I enjoy it. I minored in art, you know." She said it quietly, a hint of both pride and embarrassment in her voice.

"Then you should know these are good enough to sell. I never could picture you as a computer geek and now I see why. There's an artist hiding under all those computer codes." He leaned back against the side of the bed and rubbed his head again. The lump wasn't getting bigger, at least.

Ella sat on the edge of the mattress. Her fingers threaded through his hair, found the knot and massaged it gently. "Even geeks can have an artistic side. It's a nice outlet, but it's very personal for me. Mel's the only person who's ever seen any of my stuff—well, and you, too, now."

"All art is personal. That doesn't mean it can't be commercial, as well."

"Yeah, well…" She sighed. "It's hard to explain."

The pain in his head was subsiding, thanks to her magic touch, and he leaned forward to give her better access. "Try me."

"All of those places are special to me. It's like I have an emotional attachment to them. I guess you could say I have to love it to paint it. The thought of putting that much of me out there is…well, it's far more exposure than I'm really comfortable with."

"Emotional exposure or not, you should be doing this for a living."

"Massaging head lumps?" she teased.

"Painting."

"Believe it or not, I toyed with the thought for a while when I was younger. I even had this grand plan of moving to New Orleans after high school and living the bohemian artist's life."

"You should've." He closed his eyes and groaned as her fingers worked their way down his neck to press slightly harder on sore muscles.

Ella snorted. "Artists starve—geeks don't. Since I like to eat, I think I made the right career choice."

He pushed himself up on his knees and faced her. "But you dreamed of being an artist…"

"Matt, honey, if we all got to live our dreams, the world would be full of astronauts and rock stars. A girl's got to pay the bills."

"My dad went to a job he hated every day for thirty years just to pay the bills. There's more to life than that."

"But it's pretty important." A hard edge crept into her voice. "*My* parents were 'living their dream' when they died. They left me with nothing and my grandparents with the bills. Gran and Gramps had to give up their retirement to take me in. It's irresponsible."

He vaguely remembered something Melanie had said about Ella and her family last spring when she and Brian came to Atlanta to visit. "Yes, but—"

She held up a hand. "You said it yourself earlier—

you're working awful hours right now so you'll make partner. *Then* you'll look to settle down. SoftWerx might not be my dream job, but I worked damn hard to get there."

"But I love my job. There's the difference."

"Good for you." The cold, sarcastic tone was not one he'd ever heard from her before. A moment later she stood and walked to the other side of the room, tension radiating from her body.

A small flicker of understanding finally lit the back of his brain. "Why do I get the feeling this has something to do with the whole 'emotional abstinence' thing from earlier?"

"Spare me the chat-show analysis, okay?" she snapped before she closed her eyes and took a deep breath. "Look, if you want to believe in the fairy tale, fine. Good for you. I know firsthand that it's not that easy." She knelt beside him on the floor again and placed a small warm hand on his leg. "Let's just move on, all right? 'No messiness,' remember? I don't think amateur psychoanalysis was part of the plan."

"But, El—"

"Just drop it, okay?"

Put like that, he had no choice but to comply. He nodded and Ella grinned before she kissed him.

"We left the Chinese on the table. Go stick it in the fridge while I clean off the bed more thoroughly. I'm in the mood to try out my fortune cookie."

Once again his body won out over his brain.

* * *

Ella lay staring at the ceiling while Matt slept beside her. He'd curled himself around her, and while she was both warm and comfortable, the wandering nature of her thoughts was keeping her awake.

The past few days had been surreal, like she'd accidentally stepped into someone else's far-more-interesting life. Matt had been a godsend, uncomplainingly cheerful as he helped sort, pack and schlep the ten years' worth of stuff she and Mel had accumulated. A chore that, in retrospect, would have made her lonely and melancholy if left to do it alone.

But it hadn't been. Either by accident or design, Matt managed to keep her mind off the depressing aspect of packing memories and the reality of moving a thousand miles from the friends who'd become all the family she had. Wine, food, music and great sex—oh, yes, *lots* of great sex—kept the sobering finality of what she was doing at bay. Instead, life felt like some kind of hedonistic slumber party.

Tonight, though, the thoughts were crowding in and her chest felt tight.

"You awake?" Matt's sleep-husky voice cut through the noise in her head.

"Yeah. Sorry if I woke you."

Matt kissed her shoulder and pulled her closer, settling in to the curve of her body. "Everything okay?"

She took a deep breath, telling herself it was only a simple inquiry into her general comfort at the moment. But it didn't work. With one simple question, the last of the walls holding her together came down. The magnitude of what she was doing slammed into her, and the air left her lungs in a loud, painful rush.

Silently Matt rolled to his back, pulling her so that her head rested on his chest. Ella forced herself to breathe slowly, concentrating on calming her heartbeat to match the steady thump of his.

"Talk to me. What's wrong?"

Matt hadn't signed on to deal with her issues, and the last thing she should do—considering the nature of their relationship and her outburst earlier—was unload on him. Somehow, though, the quiet stillness and almost darkness made it easier to talk. If nothing else, she'd come to appreciate Matt's levelheadedness and clarity of thought in the past few days.

Sure, she'd weighed all the pros and cons with Melanie dozens of times before she made her decision, but maybe Mel wasn't the best source of advice in this. Mel knew what Ella wanted to hear, and Ella knew what Mel would say, so while she always felt better after an obsession session, she rarely had any new answers. Plus, Mel knew her far too well to comment with any objectivity.

Matt, on the other hand, had nothing but objectivity. As annoying as that was sometimes, it was still helpful.

"Everything is just hitting me all at once. I'm a bit overwhelmed."

"Second thoughts?"

"Not really. This job is a big step up for me. It's what I've been working toward for years, and it's a great opportunity. With SoftWerx being so close to where I grew up, I thought it was a sign or something that it was time for me to move back—especially with Mel moving out, too. But I've been here for over ten years." Once the words started, she couldn't stem the flow. "Fort Morgan is a tiny little place, and Pensacola isn't real big either. The beach is nice, and, yeah, the weather is a big plus, but what if I get bored? I haven't even been *down* there since my grandfather died."

"Then why take the job?" Matt's voice was quiet and even, soothing her.

"It's a great opportunity."

"So you said. But you don't sound overly excited about it. Surely you could get something similar here. If you're wanting to stay in Chicago, that is."

"There's really no reason to stay."

"What about your friends? What about Melanie? From what you've told me, she's the closest thing to family you've got."

"Mel's married now."

"So?"

"*So,* she's moving on. She has Brian and they're wanting to start a family right away…"

Matt shifted and turned her face to his. In the dim light of the streetlight outside her window, she could only make out some of his features, but she could tell by the shadows around his mouth that he wasn't smiling. "At the risk of practicing armchair psychology again, it sounds like you think Mel won't have time for you anymore, so you're leaving town before that happens."

Oh, God, not again. "I swear, Matt…" She untangled herself from his arms and sat up. She should've just pretended to be asleep when he asked instead of letting the melancholy get the better of her in the dark of the night.

"Hear me out. You'd rather take a job you don't really want—"

"But that's great for my career."

He levered himself to his elbows and cocked an eyebrow at her. "A career you don't sound too keen on, anyway."

Matt's tenaciousness about her job made her want to pull her hair out in frustration. What *was* his obsession with lovin' the job? "We're not going back to that 'dream job' thing again, are we?"

"Look, with your past, I'm not surprised to hear you have a fear of abandonment, but—"

"What?" This was too much—*especially* to be discussing naked in bed. Her robe still hung on the bathroom door, and she got out of bed to get it, pulling the belt tight before she faced Matt again.

Matt seemed unfazed. He had that same look he wore when they argued politics, although there was concern mixed with the challenge this time. "You talk a good game, Ella, but I'm not buying it."

This entire conversation was getting out of hand. "Why is it that women are said to have 'abandonment issues' or 'commitment issues,' but men get to be 'fiercely independent'? Men can be career driven, but if a woman is, there must be something wrong with her?"

"Don't skew the subject."

Her head was starting to hurt, and she'd now had enough. "I don't think we know each other well enough to have this discussion."

"Bull. I think we do."

That's it. "Just stop. Stop talking. I've had all the psychobabble I can handle at two in the morning." She turned on her heel and headed for the door.

"Where are you going?"

"The couch. Thanks for the offer to help, but I think it's just midnight melancholy caused by the move and I'll be better sleeping it off. Go back to sleep, Matt."

"El—"

She closed the door behind her and sighed as she sank onto the couch. She pulled an afghan around her to keep the chill at bay. Eyes closed, she leaned her head on the armrest and took deep breaths, trying to calm her temper before she really exploded. She shouldn't get all worked up over Matt's need to crawl inside her head, but it was easier said than done. Not that he was completely wrong, but, damn, it was annoying.

"Do you want me to leave?"

She opened one eye to see Matt, wearing only his boxers, leaning against the door frame to the living room. "Do you want to?"

"Not really." Matt cocked his head and smiled at her.

"But you sleeping on the couch kind of defeats the purpose of me being here."

What was left of her pique was dissipating fast. Why couldn't she stay annoyed with him? "You're right, you should be the one on the couch."

He joined her there, lifting her legs as he sat and draping them across his lap. "My brother Lewis is a therapist. I guess more of it has rubbed off than I thought."

"So we can stop this now?"

He laughed. "Lewis says I have an overinflated need to problem solve, and when I do, I am overbearing and lack subtlety."

No doubt. "You know, Lewis might be onto something there."

"Yes, but it makes me a good lawyer." He rubbed warm hands over her calves. "Now, either kick me out or come back to bed."

It was a close call. Not because she *wanted* him to leave, but because it would be much easier in the long run if she did. But she couldn't bring herself to say the magic words, since deep down, she really wanted him to stay. Once again rational thought got kicked to the curb, and she allowed Matt to lead her back to bed where, in typical annoying male fashion, he was back asleep in minutes. She, on the other hand, found sleep as elusive as ever.

Matt mumbled and rolled to his side, spooning around her. The warm arms made her feel safe. Cared for. She waited for the sense of claustrophobia to set in, the mild panic and need to get away that always came. Nothing.

Nothing except a squishy sense of contentment that relaxed her.

This wasn't good.

CHAPTER SIX

"TELL me about your brothers."

Matt looked up from the photograph he was wrapping in newsprint. "Why?"

"Because I'm curious about your family. You don't talk about them much."

He shrugged. "My family is large, loud and, thankfully, lives many, many miles from me."

"Be serious."

"I am."

She waited as he placed the photo in a box and closed the top. Matt talked about his family only in passing, and she had to admit to a burning curiosity about them. After all, he'd lied to his family in order to spend the week with her, yet when he did mention them, she heard a fondness in his voice that indicated there wasn't some kind of serious rift there. "Well?" she prodded when he didn't say anything.

"I don't know what to tell you. They're just my

family. Anyway, you seem to know quite a bit about them already."

"All I know is what Brian has told Melanie and that Melanie then mentioned to me."

"Melanie needs to worry about the family she just married into, if you ask me," Matt grumbled.

She swatted him on the arm, and he rubbed it in mock pain. "I happen to like Brian's family. Melanie's, too. Now I'm curious about yours."

"And again, I ask *why?*"

"We have to talk about something, don't we?"

"Then how about baseball?"

"I'm not going to debate Cubs versus Sox with you." She sighed. "I don't have a family. I barely remember my mom and dad, and I don't even know where my mom's family is. Dad was an only child, so Gran and Gramps were the only family I had growing up. The idea of having a large family just…" *Whoa.* That was a lot more information than she normally shared, and she wasn't sure what had brought on that revelation. She cleared her throat. "Meeting Melanie's family was quite a shock, and it's not even that big."

"Meeting Brian's must have been a real eye-opener, then."

"Brian's family is like something out of a movie. Since y'all are from the same neighborhood, I just wondered if yours was like his or not." She shrugged. "But if you don't want to talk about them, I'll respect that."

"You'll 'respect' that?" He laughed.

"Of course." She put on her sweetest smile and best Southern accent. "Unlike some people, I don't push others to tell me details they don't wish to share or pry into things that aren't my business."

He snorted. "I can tell you're not from a big family. Pushing and prying are part of the deal."

She continued to smile at him until he rolled his eyes and sighed. "Fine. We'll talk about my family."

Matt continued to wrap knickknacks as he talked, explaining family dynamics in a way she'd never thought about before. While it was obvious his family irritated and annoyed him and he had a slew of complaints stemming from being the youngest child, it was equally obvious that he cared deeply about his entire extended family and remained close—at least emotionally if not physically—to his brothers and parents.

That explained a lot about Matt's attitude toward life. He had a safety net. He didn't need to worry about "what might happen if…" It was easy to not be a control freak when someone else had your back.

"Hell, El, you did ask."

She tuned back in to see Matt's exasperated look. "I'm sorry, what?"

"You're the one who wanted to talk about my family, but then you space out?"

"Your family sounds great."

"They'd like you, too. If I wouldn't give my mom a heart attack showing up at the house after telling her I was going back to Atlanta, I'd take you to meet them.

My dad has a thing for Southern accents and my mom is a great cook. In short spells and small groupings, they're really quite tolerable."

She shifted uncomfortably at the thought of meeting his family. That wasn't part of the plan. She quickly changed direction. "You know, I'm feeling guilty for keeping you here instead of letting you spend time with them."

Newsprint scattered as Matt closed the space between them. "Ah, but you're far more interesting than my family. Better-looking, too." He punctuated his words with a kiss that curled her toes.

Lifting his head, he looked around the living room. "Well, this room is pretty much done, so what say we take a break?"

She followed his gaze around the room. Books still lined the bookshelves and sat in crooked piles. Photos and knickknacks—mostly belonging to Melanie—still needed to be wrapped and packed. "This room is nowhere near done."

"Close enough." He nuzzled her neck. "And after moving all that furniture earlier, I really need a shower. Care to join me?"

Visions of a wet, soapy Matt blinded her, and she giggled as he hauled her to her feet and tugged her in the direction of the bathroom. She shimmied out of her jeans as Matt turned the water on.

"You have the smallest shower in the city. It's going to be a tight fit."

"That doesn't sound like a bad thing to me," she

answered as she stepped in and pulled the shower curtain closed. Only inches separated them.

Matt moved her under the shower spray and traced the water rivulets over her breasts with his finger. "You're right. Not bad at all."

Grabbing the bar of soap, she built up a handful of lather and smoothed suds across Matt's chest. The look that crossed his face as he reached for her promised this would be the best shower of her life.

Granted, at this rate, she'd never get the apartment packed in time, but for once she wasn't going to let her plans get in the way of her pleasure.

Somehow everything got packed, and she was ready when the moving men arrived Friday morning. The flurry of activity caused by four men traipsing through her apartment and loading her life onto a truck kept her busy and her mind off what all the activity meant.

But after the moving truck left, the apartment felt lifeless. Aside from the few boxes and some furniture left for Melanie's brothers to pick up and take to Brian's, every room felt empty and echoing. Ella sat against the living-room wall with Matt, approximately where her couch used to be, eating the last real Chicago dog she'd have for quite a while.

She concentrated on her food, enjoying the taste and textures, because if her mind wandered for more than a second, tears began to burn behind her eyes. Ella kept telling herself it was the move and not the complication of the man sitting next to her.

Occasionally she almost believed herself.

Matt had been unusually quiet all morning, and for the first time since they'd met, conversation seemed stilted. Maybe that was a good thing—a sign that they'd run their course and the goodbyes would be easier. The goodbyes were not something she was looking forward to this time.

"You know, Atlanta's not that far from Fort Morgan."

She swallowed the last bite before she answered. "Like seven hours."

"Or an hour by plane."

Ella gathered up the garbage and took a last swallow of her drink. "I thought we'd covered this already. We agreed it only went this far—any further wouldn't be a good idea."

Matt eased over into her space, pushing her slowly to the floor. One leg captured hers and he twirled a lock of hair around his finger. Ella flashed back to the first night he'd been in her apartment, and they'd been in almost the exact same position in this same place on the floor. Except last time, there'd been a rug between her and the hardwood.

"I beg to differ. I didn't agree to anything of the sort."

"What happened to 'you'll go on with your life and I'll go back to mine'?"

"Ahh, the words of a man trying to have his cake and eat it, too. That was before I got used to you, Ella. You're addictive."

Her heart slammed into her chest at his words. This was going to be much harder than she'd thought. So much for not getting messy. In fact, this was getting messier by the minute. She tried to keep her voice light. "Still, Atlanta's a little far for me to come for a booty call."

Matt's eyes hardened, and his mouth tightened a tiny bit in what she recognized now as disappointment. But to her surprise, he let her comment go. "My firm gets tickets to all the best shows. And they're not lousy seats, either. REM is playing next month—why don't you come up for a few days?"

He'd teased her endlessly about her obsession with them, and between the allure of tickets and the promising movement of his hips, the temptation was almost over-whelming. "I don't think my new employers would appre-ciate me taking a few days off just weeks after I start."

In one swift motion her shirt was whisked over her head. Matt's lips landed on her collarbone, making her rethink his proposal as he worked the snap on her jeans. "Priorities, El," he mumbled as his mouth sought hers. His hands moved with amazing efficiency, unhooking her bra, sliding her jeans over her hips, and in moments her bare skin touched the cool floor.

Once she was naked, though, Matt's movements slowed and his hands worked slow, agonizing magic over her skin. This was no last quickie for the road, and as always he was able to remove her ability to think ra-tionally. She quit trying and gave over to the sensation of his body against hers.

Her skin was on fire from his touch, and she was seconds from begging when he finally thrust into her. She arched, pleasure rocketing through her, and she locked her legs around his waist, ready for him to take her the rest of the way.

Matt stilled and she reached for his hips. This was no time for him to tease—she was too close, too needy. When he didn't move, she opened her eyes to find him staring intently at her. Those chocolate eyes pinned her, and her stomach clenched.

"This isn't over, Ella."

With that statement his mouth closed over hers, and he moved in her with deep strokes that caused stars to explode behind her eyelids. Pleasure crashed against the shock of his words, and she fought to make sense of the feeling. Matt groaned her name into her ear, and the response that rocketed through her brought a clarity that both excited and terrified her.

He'd said it wasn't over.

It had to be.

"I've got to go, Matt." Ella wiggled out of his embrace and glanced at her watch. "I'm serious this time."

She'd been saying that for the past two hours, but she hadn't made any real progress for the door. While he knew she had a long drive ahead of her, he'd been reluctant to see her go and tried every stalling technique he could think of to keep her from leaving. The empty hours between now and his flight tomorrow loomed, and he selfishly wanted Ella to stay as long as possible.

Ella seemed to mean it this time as she pulled on socks and shoes, keeping a careful distance between them the whole time. Defeated in his attempt to stall her, he buttoned his shirt and reached for his shoes.

He stood, then extended a hand to pull her to her feet. Silence settled over them, and she shifted uncomfortably.

"Well, um, okay." She took a deep breath. "I guess that's everything. Just leave the keys at Brian's, and that'll take care of the apartment."

"No problem." Ella wouldn't meet his eyes, and that bothered him. "Do you have your cell?"

She sighed. "Yes. And my Triple-A card. I'm a big girl, Matt. I can handle this."

"I know. It's just such a long drive." He didn't like the thought of her making it alone. "Has your car been checked out? Oil? Tires?"

"Oh, for God's sake." Sighing dramatically, Ella turned on her heel and headed for the stairs.

He was right behind her. "Seriously. Has it been looked over?"

Ella made it to her car before he caught up with her. She still wouldn't answer him, so he crossed his arms over his chest and leaned his hip against the driver's door, making it impossible for her to open it. She tried several times anyway. His size did give him an advantage when it came to dealing with her.

"Ella? Did you get this car checked out?"

"I swear. Do you really think I'm an idiot?" She looked at him pointedly, but when he still wouldn't budge, she conceded. "Be that way. Yes, Matt, I did. Just last week it got a full going-over. At your brother's shop, I might add." Her eyebrows went up in challenge.

That mollified him some. Josh wouldn't let her go on the road if the car wouldn't make it.

"Satisfied?"

Not by a long shot. But he shifted his weight off the car's door so she could open it and toss her purse inside. He half expected her to jump in and roar off, but she leaned against the car and studied him, squinting against the afternoon sun.

Ella zipped her jacket and stuck her hands in the pockets. "So this is it."

"I guess so."

"You made this week bearable for me, and I don't know how to thank you for that."

"Then don't." He didn't want her gratitude. He opened his arms, and she walked into them without hesitation. *That* was more like it.

With her head pressed into his chest, her voice was muffled. "I just don't know how to say goodbye."

The finality in her voice caught him off guard. "You make it sound so permanent," he said carefully.

"Honestly, Matt, I think it is."

He kept his voice even. "Why?"

"Be realistic."

Ella was complicated, but he'd figured out a lot

about her over the past week. She had issues—some ran pretty deep—but he could respect that. God knew he had a few of his own, but he'd never met anyone like her before and wasn't willing to just pretend the past week never happened.

But she couldn't wait for him to be just a reflection in her rearview mirror. Not exactly a big boost to his ego.

He chose his words with care. He didn't want to spook her. "It's unrealistic that we could be friends?"

Ella sighed. "Not necessarily unrealistic. Just really complicated."

She had a point there. "Yeah, well, Atlanta is—"

"'Only an hour away.' I know." Ella laughed and leaned back to look at him. "But I actually meant Melanie."

Of all the possible "complications," Melanie had never crossed his mind. "What does Melanie have to do with anything?"

"I don't want Mel to know about us. What happened this week, I mean. Unless you want Mel planning your wedding with or without your consent, it's best she not know we hooked up. She's gotten very self-righteous in her old age, you know."

"You're an adult, Ella. You don't need Mel's permission."

"Yes, but messy won't even begin to describe…"

"If that's the only issue, it's easily enough solved. Don't tell her."

"But Mel would—"

He wanted to shake some sense into her. "We've got

something really interesting here, El. I'm not asking you to marry me or anything, but I don't want to just slam the door and pretend we never met."

"A friends-with-benefits sort of thing?"

Only Ella could come up with that kind of terminology. The girl was the queen of keeping herself at a distance. "For now you could call it that."

He could feel her hesitation.

"Well, that's... I mean, it could be..."

Not wanting to push her, he just let her stammer on while he rubbed circles over the tense muscles of her back. After a long moment she leaned back and smiled up at him.

"You've got my number. Call me sometime and we'll see what happens."

Well, it was something. He returned the smile, then leaned in to kiss her. Just as the kiss started to heat up, tempting him to carry her right back up the stairs, she broke away.

"I *have* to go. But this has been one heck of a send-off."

His body rebelled at her words, but he released her. "Then go. Drive carefully, El."

She honked as she drove away, and Matt debated what he'd do with the rest of his time in Chicago. A week ago he'd had big plans of late nights out with the old crowd and drinking beer with his brothers, but now he was having a hard time dredging up much interest.

That in itself was odd.

He locked Ella's apartment and walked the six blocks to Brian's. He couldn't call his brothers—the family thought he was in Atlanta, and he'd have a devil of a time trying to explain to his mother why he lied and avoided them all week.

His phone vibrated in his pocket, startling him. He'd had it off since Sunday and only just turned it on this morning. He hadn't even checked to see how many calls he'd missed or how many messages were waiting for him. He'd been so caught up in Ella, he'd completely forgotten everything waiting for him at the office. With his firm's number showing in the display, the real world came rushing back.

His assistant was on the other end, practically frantic. "Where the *hell* have you been? I was about to call the Chicago PD and file a missing persons report."

The lazy, relaxed feeling he'd grown used to this week began to evaporate. "Long story, Debbie. What's up?"

"What's *up?*" Debbie's voice rose two octaves as she spoke. "You drop off the face of the earth in the middle of the Cooper contracts and never call to check in and you're asking *me* what's up?"

And with that, his vacation was officially over.

As the Chicago skyline retreated in her rearview mirror, Ella had time to think. Away from the intoxicating confusion Matt created just by breathing near her, she sought clarity.

It was slow in coming.

Matt's sudden eagerness to pretend there could be something between them—even if it was just basically being bed buddies—confused her at first, but once the afterglow of good sex began to fade, she started to understand. Well, somewhat.

Trying to reconcile the Matt she'd heard about for years with the Matt she'd just spent the week with was enough to make her head hurt. Aside from the fact she didn't seem like Matt's type, Mel had claimed—and even Matt substantiated it—that he was a workaholic and in no hurry to commit to anyone.

Which, now that she was thinking clearly, ex-plained *so* much. She was "safe"—no threat at all to his current lifestyle or his plans to make partner and find a nice girl to settle down with sometime in five years or so.

Maybe *that* was why she was open to his ideas. After all, he wouldn't expect much from her, so she'd never have to worry he'd want more than what she was able to give. He was pretty "safe" for her as well.

Traveling that hour on a plane for a little sexual release once in a while was starting to sound like a pretty good idea. Maybe she could keep Melanie and Brian in the dark and eliminate the messiness factor.

Who am I kidding? Once Matt gets home, he'll real-ize we were nothing more than a fling and move on. He would forget about her soon enough and go back to his grand five-year plan.

Trying to be objective, she told herself that would be the better development. No muss, no fuss.

Then why didn't it feel that way?

She shook her head. Since when did she have this appalling need to self-psychoanalyze?

Why hadn't she stayed with her earlier plan instead of telling him to call her sometime? She'd been trying to avoid messiness and here she was smack in the middle of it.

She had to get control of herself or else she was going to need real therapy.

City and suburbs had given way to trees and hills without her noticing, and she was surprised to see the big sign welcoming her to Kentucky.

She rolled down her window and let the cool evening air blow over her and chase away the fog in her head. *This* was reality. She was headed home and to a new part of her life. The past week would make for a fun memory, but it had a golden tint *because* it wasn't really real— just an interlude in an otherwise normal life.

It had been fun. Amazing, actually. But she had to be realistic.

No harm, no foul. No one's heart got broken, and no one's feelings got hurt.

Now she just had to work on forgetting him.

CHAPTER SEVEN

ELLA walked along the beach enjoying the last warm rays of the sun as it sank below the horizon. The waves lapped at her feet, the water of the Gulf of Mexico cooling as the temperatures caught up with the calendar. Roscoe, her neighbor's eight-month-old Great Dane puppy, joined her as usual, bounding ahead to bark at sandpipers and seagulls before circling back to hurry her along. It was the Friday after Halloween and summer was officially over, but there were still a few tourists on the beach taking advantage of the just-warm-enough weather and off-season rates to grab one last long weekend before the winter set in and the snowbirds arrived from up north.

The thought of the influx of winter residents from the snow-laden states made her think of Chicago and Mel, which quickly led her thoughts to one particular Yankee transplant. Not that Matt had been far from her mind at all in the past three weeks; he had a way of sneaking in no matter what else she tried to focus on.

She'd dived headfirst into her new job just two days after the moving truck left, figuring work would be the best cure for the homesickness that niggled at her late at night. But while SoftWerx challenged her, it didn't bring any sort of satisfaction, and she blamed Matt for sowing discontent in her chosen career field.

It didn't help that Matt turned out to be serious about that "let's be friends" thing. Although he never called, he did send fun, flirty e-mails pinging into her in-box, and much to her own amazement, she'd begun to look forward to seeing his name in the return-address field. She'd even flirted back, enjoying it.

Well, until last week, at least, when Matt told her he was going to a meeting in New Orleans and asked her to make the drive over for the weekend. *That* had pretty much stopped her in her electronic tracks. Matt was safe to flirt with when he was in Atlanta, but seeing him again wasn't something she was quite ready to deal with just yet.

"What do you think, Roscoe? Should I have gone to New Orleans?" The black puppy trotted tiredly beside her on this last leg back to the house, but looked up when she said his name. She patted his head. "It's a tough call, I know."

Roscoe wasn't helpful, but he had been a good listener on these walks, particularly when it came to the confusing nature of her feelings for Matt.

She liked him. He liked her. For someone else, it would be so easy. *Ha.* Each e-mail moved her a little closer into dangerous territory. They were close to becoming actual friends now. That wasn't what she'd planned on.

Instead of forgetting him, she was getting to know him better and she was constantly being reminded of the guy who had almost made her let down her guard.

That guard—the one Melanie kept dogging her about—was what had kept her sane and grounded all her life. Matt was a loose cannon in her otherwise orderly life. He was a nice interlude, a fantasy that had been fun to explore, but the reality was far too complicated to contemplate.

And that was the exact reason she *hadn't* agreed to meet Matt in New Orleans. His invitation had been a wake-up call, reminding her of her earlier intention to limit any contact with Matt whatsoever. And, more important, *why* she'd come to that decision. She'd claimed she was too busy at SoftWerx to get away, but it was a flimsy excuse, and she figured he'd seen straight through it.

"Too late now, right, Roscoe?"

But Roscoe ignored her, not even perking up his ears at the mention of his name. Then, with a bark that belied his usual playful puppyness, he took off across the boardwalk toward her house behind the dunes.

From her vantage point on the boardwalk, she could see her back porch and the man standing on it who had caught Roscoe's attention. A lost tourist, probably. It wasn't uncommon for tourists to get lost and end up knocking on her door looking for their vacation rental. Heck, she'd even had a couple try to move in—locks were important around here for that simple reason.

Roscoe's barking gained the man's attention, and he turned in the direction of the sound. She watched as he spotted the dog first, then traced Roscoe's path in the direction of the beach to where she was stepping off the boardwalk. She was finally able to get a good look at the man, and when she did her heart skipped a beat.

Matt. What on earth was he doing here?

She struggled to find her equilibrium as he called out a greeting to her. She wanted to be angry that he was here without an invitation—especially since she'd turned down *his* invitation for the weekend—but part of her was thrilled.

"Hey, El."

Be cool. "Hi, yourself." She accepted the quick kiss on her cheek before adding, "What are you doing here?"

Matt laughed. "Nice to see you, too. I— Ooph!"

Roscoe, still barking with excitement, jumped on Matt, both paws landing squarely in Matt's crotch. After grabbing the dog's paws and dropping them gently to the ground, Matt squatted to pet the slobbering dog without exposing himself to clumsy puppy feet. Roscoe reveled in the attention, rolling onto his back to give Matt access to his tummy. When Matt complied, Roscoe's big head lolled back in doggie delight.

I know exactly how you feel, Roscoe.

"Who's this?"

"That's Roscoe. He belongs to Molly across the street. He tags along when I walk on the beach." At the sound of her voice, Roscoe seemed to remember where his loyalty should lie, and he scrambled back to his feet to stand at her side. She pointed her finger at the blue cottage almost identical to her own. "Go home, boy."

Head drooping, Roscoe obeyed.

Brushing sand and dog hair from his jeans, Matt stood. "Nice place."

She crossed her arms and leaned against the porch railing. "At the risk of sounding rude, I'll ask you again. What are you doing here?"

Matt cocked an eyebrow at her. "Well, if Mohammed won't come to the mountain…"

"I told you I was busy this weekend. Work, you know."

"Yes, and you're a terrible liar—even by e-mail."

So he'd figured that out, too. She shrugged and dug the door key from her pocket. "I never realized I was so transparent."

"It's just part of my job, ma'am." He grinned. "It's a lawyer thing."

The smug look on Matt's face bordered on smack-able, but he was just too cute to deny. And since she could admit to herself, at least, that she was glad to see him—even if it did cause heart flutters—she opened the door and ushered him in.

Matt's eyes widened at the mess that greeted him, and she smothered a chuckle. The furniture was in place, but the stacks of boxes, barren shelves and blank walls seemed to catch him off guard.

"Lord, El. Am I going to have to *un*pack you, as well?"

That did cause a chuckle. "Hmm, the free labor is tempting. Especially since you did such a good job packing those boxes. But, no. I'm having some work done on the house, now that I'll be living here full-time, and there's no sense unpacking before the contractors arrive. Would you like something to drink?"

He nodded, and the mindless task of playing hostess gave her something to do with herself. Matt's presence seemed to cause the room to shrink, and it felt like the heat had kicked on. *Distance,* she thought. *Distance is what I need.* The bar counter separating the kitchen from the living room was a flimsy barrier, but she seemed to breathe a bit easier with it between them.

Matt stood on the other side of the counter and nodded at the roll of house plans. "I can't believe you'd jump right in to house renovations. I would've thought you'd want to settle in first."

"Gran and Gramps always wanted to expand this place—add another bedroom, extend the porch and screen part of it in, redo the kitchen—but they never seemed to have the money. Gramps had those plans drawn up years ago, but something always came up and it never got done. This job at SoftWerx finally means I'll have the money to do what Gramps wanted." Matt was watching her closely, so she hurried on. "No time like the present, right?"

"So the job's going well?"

She plastered a smile on her face. "Oh, yeah. I'm really busy and there's a learning curve to navigate, but it's really challenging and a really great opportunity."

Matt smirked. "Really?"

Stop babbling. Damn Matt anyway for rattling her about her job. She needed to get control of herself and make actual conversation. "You know what? I'm hungry. If you're here for a visit, why don't we go get some dinner? I'd offer to cook, but once again, you've caught me with my cupboards bare."

"I kinda like catching you 'bare.'"

Heat rushed to her cheeks and at the same time desire curled through her belly. It was a strange combination. Only Matt could embarrass her and turn her on at the same time.

"I know a great place. Let me go get changed." She forced herself to walk calmly to her room. As she shut the door behind her, she suppressed the urge to bang her head against it. This was insane. She wasn't supposed to be seeing Matt anymore.

What a mess.

Dinner. Dinner would be safe. She could get her head screwed back on straight and decide what to do next.

Fifteen minutes later she knew exactly how wrong she was. Placing herself in the close confines of Matt's sports car was a monumental mistake. Why couldn't he have gotten a regular rental like normal people? Something midsize, with plenty of space inside. *No.* Matt rented a little red sports car, which meant his big body took up a great deal of the front seat. She was close enough to feel the heat radiating off his skin, and if she moved too much, her arm slid against his, raising all the tiny hairs on her arm from the contact.

To make matters worse, the faintest whiff of his scent clung to the inside of the car, and every time she inhaled, she got light-headed at the rush.

She tried to sit very still and breathe shallowly through her mouth.

"Are you okay?"

Not in the least. "Fine. The restaurant is just up on your left."

She was out of the car the second it stopped moving, not even waiting for him to come around and open her door. Matt arched an eyebrow at her quizzically, but said nothing as they walked in.

The hostess showed them to a battered booth, and she slid in to her side, grateful for the table's width between them. But when Matt's long legs bumped hers, she knew it was going to be the longest meal of her life.

She flagged down their server.

"I'd like a very large, very cold, very *strong* margarita, please."

Of all the ideas Matt had about what he would do once he and Ella were together again, battling seafood wasn't one of them. His visions always centered on Ella naked and writhing beneath him, those gorgeous legs of hers wrapped around his waist as he slammed into her.

Instead the only legs he was fondling at the moment were hard and spiny and formerly attached to a crab.

Ella had been a nice distraction once he returned to Atlanta and his assistant dumped a pile of paperwork on his desk. Firing off e-mails took no time at all and provided a break when he needed one. She never initiated contact, but she always replied to his messages. It was a simple, easy friendship, but he spent far too much time thinking about her.

He'd been more than a little disappointed at her refusal to meet him in New Orleans this weekend. The mere idea had filled him with enough erotic fantasies to cause possible embarrassment if his mind wandered during a meeting. While Ella might be surprised at him for showing up on her front porch, he couldn't be that close to her and not at least try to see her.

But he hadn't been prepared for the need to get her to the nearest horizontal surface that had hit into him the moment she appeared on the boardwalk. If it hadn't been for that puppy's unerring aim...

Instead he found himself sitting in a restaurant that could best be described as a dive, wrestling his dinner out of its shell.

"Hold this side and twist when you pull. You'll starve to death before you get enough meat out doing it your way." In demonstration, Ella deftly pulled the crab leg apart, and the meat slid out in one perfect piece. She dipped it in butter and popped it in her mouth. She closed her eyes, savoring the taste. "Yum."

His body reacted instantly. He'd seen a variant of that look directed at him. As her tongue snaked out to lick a drop of butter from her bottom lip, sweat broke out on his brow and he shifted uncomfortably. The woman even made shellfish erotic. Enough small talk. He needed to get her out of here. *Now.* He reached for his wallet.

"How's work?" she asked, completely unaware of the thoughts in his head.

The question stopped him from doing the ridiculous and dragging Ella out of the restaurant by her hair, caveman-style. He settled into his seat and reached for his beer, hoping the cool drink would magically cool his libido.

"About the same. Busy."

Ella shook her head. "You work too hard. Too many long hours in the office isn't good for a person, you know. Fresh air is important."

"I'm getting some now. What could be fresher than a sea breeze?"

She ran her finger along the edge of her glass and licked the salt away, tormenting him further. "Still, I can't think of *anything* I'd be willing to do for sixty or seventy hours a week. No matter how enjoyable."

Heat moved through him again. The beer wasn't helping. He waited until he caught her eye, then held her gaze far too long before moving his eyes deliberately downward. When he finally returned to her face, her pupils were dilated and color flagged her cheeks.

"I can think of something."

He heard Ella's breath catch, and she looked away. A split second later, he heard her signal for the server.

"Check, please."

Need bordering on pain flooded in, displacing the flash of disappointment he'd felt when she'd broken eye contact. He fished out his wallet and threw a stack of bills on the table. Grabbing Ella's hand, he scooted out of the booth and sprinted for the parking lot with her in tow.

Ella slid into the passenger seat of his rental as he cranked the engine. Unable to wait any longer, he dragged her into his lap and found her lips. She moaned, pouring gasoline on the flames licking him.

In the past week, he'd decided he was remembering Chicago wrong—that no woman could taste that good or feel so perfect in his arms. But the reality proved the memory true. He reached for the seat control, reclining the back and giving them more room.

His hands found the hem of her T-shirt and slid under to feel the soft skin of her belly contract at his touch. Ella's nails dug into his shoulders as his fingers moved higher to find the swell of breast above the lace-edged cup of her bra. She hissed, arching into his hand, and the hard point of her nipple pressed into his palm. She rocked against him, and he grabbed hold of her hips to increase the friction.

She was fumbling with the snap of his jeans when loud catcalls and a thump on the hood brought him forcefully back to reality. Three teenage boys stood in front of the car, whistling and making suggestions.

Sanity returned. Sweet heaven, he was seconds from taking her in the front seat of a car in a parking lot like some horny high-schooler.

Five minutes. He would have to hold on for the five minutes it would take to get her back to the house.

Ignoring Ella's moan of protest, he moved her back to her seat and threw the car into gear.

Ella's hand snaked into his lap to rest on his thigh, only inches from the part of his anatomy controlling him at the moment. Her fingers moved slightly, causing the muscle in his thigh to jump. He tightened his hands on the steering wheel, trying to concentrate on the road. "Dammit, Ella! Are you trying to get us killed?"

In the darkness of the car, he heard her whisper, "Hurry."

The gravel in her driveway crunched under the tires and he slammed the gearshift into Park. Ella was already out of the car and turning the key in the lock as he caught up.

The lock disengaged, and the door swung open. Scooping Ella up in one arm, he closed the door with the other as her mouth clamped on his.

Those legs finally wrapped around his waist, and she murmured, "First door on the left," against his lips as her fingers threaded through his hair.

Ella's bedroom. Thank heaven. Two more steps and he wouldn't have to worry about taking her on the floor.

The bed groaned as they landed on it. Ella struggled

to her knees, tugging at the hem of her T-shirt. In one swift movement he had his shirt over his head, and with his assistance her shirt and bra joined it on the floor a second later. Ella's head dropped back when his hands cupped her breasts, and she grabbed his shoulders for support as he thumbed her nipples to quivering peaks. When his mouth replaced his fingers, her nails scored across his back.

"Matt," she whispered.

The husky sound of his name on her lips scorched through him. It was easy enough to sweep her off her knees and onto her back where he quickly freed her from her jeans.

He ran his hands across the smooth skin of her hips, reacquainting himself with the feel of her as Ella's hands worked fast at his zipper. Then it was his turn to groan as delicate fingers wrapped firmly around him, sending hot bolts of lightning through his veins.

Pulling Ella under him, he whispered an apology in advance. "This won't be slow and easy."

"Good," she panted, and his heart thudded in his chest.

Ella was wet and warm as he slid into her. He struggled to keep his sanity as she moved beneath him, matching his rhythm. He felt the tiny shudders begin, heard the breathy moans that meant she was close.

Her hands fisted in the sheets and she arched against him, shouting his name and pushing him over the edge.

His last clear thought, though, would've sent Ella running for the door.

* * *

The shifting of the bed woke her up. Exhausted from more than three hours of nonstop sex, she'd finally fallen asleep around midnight, overly aware of Matt's big body taking up a large portion of her bed.

Again.

In an odd way she didn't want to examine too closely, it felt perfectly natural to have him next to her. Not that her bed had felt empty or anything, but it had felt strange to sleep alone after sharing a bed with him. When Matt eased out from under the covers, she knew it. When he didn't return within a few minutes, she rolled to her side and pried her eyes open. Searching the dark room, she saw him in front of the sliding door of her bedroom, looking out over the beach.

"Whatcha doing?"

He started at her voice, then came to kneel at the edge of the bed. He had put on his jeans, she noticed, but nothing else. Her mouth watered at the sight of his broad chest, shocking her a little. After several mind-blowing orgasms, she should be all sexed out.

Obviously not.

Moonlight streamed in through the glass, giving Matt a slightly otherworldly glow as he stroked her hair back out of her face.

"I didn't mean to wake you."

"It's fine. What were you looking at?"

"The beach. The moon's bright enough to make the sand glow. Pretty cool."

She nodded in agreement.

Matt leaned on his elbows, causing the bed to dip and making her roll slightly toward him. "Why don't we go for a walk on the beach?"

"A walk?" Surely she hadn't heard him correctly. At his enthusiastic nod, she glanced blearily at the clock. "It's three o'clock in the morning."

"But there's a full moon and you're not sleeping anyway."

"It wouldn't kill either of us to try," she grumbled.

"Come on. It'll be romantic."

Matt was obviously keen on this walk idea. She needed sleep, but since he'd done everything short of turn her inside out to pleasure her this evening, she could humor him on this.

"All right." She stretched, then gathered her clothes from the floor. "But I'm sleeping late tomorrow morning, and I expect you to cook breakfast."

"Deal." Matt broke into a brilliant smile and she realized she couldn't stay grumpy at him for long.

The night breeze coming off the water was cool, and she grabbed a sweatshirt to pull over her head as they headed toward the beach. At the head of the boardwalk, Roscoe appeared like magic, barking happily.

"Shh, you'll wake the neighborhood." The puppy sped away down the steps, reappearing as an inky spot on the snow-white beaches ahead. He barked as if encouraging them to hurry.

Matt reached for her hand and held it as they walked comfortably in silence. Occasionally a crab, glowing white under the moon, would skitter across the sand toward a wave, but other than Roscoe, they were alone on the beach. It was quite romantic, like something out of a movie, and she felt as if they were the only two people on earth at the moment.

Matt broke the silence first. "Is it always this quiet down here at night?"

"Pretty much. It's almost all residential this far down the beach. The rentals are all houses—no condos or hotels, you'll notice—so we mostly get families. The college kids like to stay farther up the beach in Gulf Shores, so we miss a lot of that noise and hassle. This time of year, though, it's mostly just locals, and *they* are asleep at three in the morning," she finished pointedly.

Roscoe came bounding back to check on them, circling once and nudging her hand for a pat of affection before heading off to sniff in the sand dunes.

"You think you could get him to go home?" Matt asked suddenly.

She blinked at the strange change of topic. "It's doubtful. Why? Don't you like dogs?"

"I like dogs just fine, but I hadn't counted on having one for company just now. He's cramping my style."

"Oh, please. What style?"

She was treated to an overdramatic sigh that was quite amusing coming from a big guy like Matt.

"A beautiful moonlit night on the beach, a beautiful woman... My plans involved seducing you and making love on the beach in the moonlight, but that's very hard to do with Roscoe about."

Don't laugh. She bit her lip, but Matt looked so exasperated that a small giggle escaped anyway. "You tourist boys. You've watched way too many movies. The last place on earth you'd want to have sex is on the beach. You get sand in all sorts of uncomfortable places."

Matt arched that eyebrow at her, making her want to yank it back down. "And you know this from personal experience?"

"As a teenager, I did my fair share of making out on the beach—mostly with tourist boys who had the same notion as you. In theory, it's great, but the reality is scratchy. My friend Sara used to call it 'sandpaper sex.'" Matt winced, and she nodded. "So Roscoe or no Roscoe, there's no way you're getting lucky out here. At least not with me, that is."

"Another horribly romantic idea killed by your pragmatism."

"Sorry." She rose up on tiptoe to kiss him. "But walking is nice, too. You can get lucky back at the house later."

Matt perked up at that. "I'll race you."

"Very funny."

"Come on, you're the track star. Let's see you run."

She couldn't resist the challenge in his voice, and she took off down the beach. Running on sand was tough on her knees and ankles, but she quickly put distance between her and Matt. Roscoe, yapping excitedly at the change of events, ran at her side, and they both beat Matt to the boardwalk by a full half-minute.

"Damn, girl, you are fast." He sat on the wooden

stairs with a loud groan. "I guess I need to add more cardio to my workout." He took deep gulping breaths before adding, "You don't happen to have a defibrillator at the house, do you?"

Ella massaged a burning thigh muscle, unable to dredge up any sympathy. "You're the one who wanted to race, tough guy. It's not my fault your ego had to take a beating." She took a deep breath herself. "I'm so out of shape."

"Your shape looks pretty good to me."

"Flattery will get you everywhere." She was feeling magnanimous after her win. "Let's go in. I need a drink of water, and you can throw a few more compliments my way." As Matt pulled himself to his feet with a groan, she added, "I may have shot down your romantic *From Here to Eternity* moment, but I can offer you a hammock on the side porch with a nice view of the ocean."

"A hammock, you say?"

"It's romantic, yet it has a degree of difficulty built in. You interested?"

"Very," he said, as he took off briskly toward the house, leaving her standing where she was and feeling slightly bewildered.

He was halfway to the house when she heard, "Race you!"

"Men," she muttered.

CHAPTER EIGHT

"I CAN'T believe I didn't know how much fun a hammock could be." Matt dropped one long leg over the side and set the hammock gently swinging.

Ella laughed as she snuggled closer under the quilt covering them both. Once the sun went down, the temperatures dropped dramatically, and she was thankful for the warmth radiating off him. "Glad to know I'm providing new experiences for you."

There were worse ways to spend a Saturday. She thought back to the many plans she'd had for today—boring work around the house, mostly—all traded for a easy day of listening to the surf while lying half-naked in Matt's arms. Once again, Matt managed to turn her life from predicable to decadent with one lazy grin.

She didn't want to move from the warm cocoon where she was idly tracing circles on Matt's chest, but the grumble in her stomach meant they'd have to search for dinner soon enough.

"My neighbor runs an art gallery."

"Hmm." She didn't want pizza, but what else could she get delivered out here?

"I was telling her about you. She's willing to take a look if you'll send her some pictures of your stuff."

Her hand stilled. "What?"

"She says they're always looking for new artists, and if she likes what she sees—and I know she will—she'll show it in the gallery."

The thought of having her art in an Atlanta gallery sent a jolt through her. That was the stuff of pipe dreams; she knew she wasn't good enough to make *that* leap.

"That's sweet of you, but I'm not quite gallery material."

"Why do you say that?"

She cleared her throat. "You have many fine qualities and a decent knowledge of art, but that doesn't necessarily make you qualified to evaluate it." She patted his arm to lighten the moment. "Stick to lawyering."

Matt tried to sit up, sending the hammock swaying dangerously and destroying the warm cocoon she'd built. She grabbed for the edge to keep from flipping out, then wrapped the quilt around her shoulders.

"And who else has been 'evaluating' your work recently?"

"What?"

"Seems to me that if you're not putting your stuff out there, you don't have much of an idea of whether you're any good or not."

She sighed. "Matt, I know enough—"

"And I say you're not the best judge of your own work." Matt fished a business card out of his back pocket. "Send some slides to Gillian. See what she says. What do you have to lose?"

Only my pride. "I told you, it's just a hobby."

"But you'll never know unless you try. Take the chance, El." A smirk of challenge curled across his face. "I dare you."

Oh, for Pete's sake. "You *dare* me? Are we back in junior high? You sound twelve."

"Damn it, El. Take a chance for once and quit being so damn careful about everything. You can't be totally in control all the time. Sometimes you just have to let go and see what happens."

There was a heated undertone in his voice she didn't understand. Something other than just her paintings had him worked up. She swung her legs over the side of the hammock and stood, making Matt grasp for the ropes this time to keep from landing flat on the porch.

"What *exactly* are we talking about now?"

Matt hesitated, and the silence stretched out between them. Finally he sat on the edge of the hammock and braced his feet on the weathered boards. He raised an eyebrow. "Us."

Shock slammed into her. "Us? Like with a capital *U?* I didn't think there's an 'Us' to be discussing."

"And whose fault is that?"

Good lord, the boy was frustrating. "Now there's 'fault'? You've lost me, Matt."

"Don't even try to play ignorant. You're a lot smarter than that, and I think you know exactly what I'm talking about."

You know you do, a little voice inside her said. With Matt, though, there was no telling where his brain was, and no sense in arguing with him, either. "I'm going in and ordering pizza. Are you hungry?"

She was barely inside the house before Matt caught her arm. Damn his long legs.

"Avoidance? Changing the subject? Come on, Ella, I expected more from you."

That tripped her trigger. "What *do* you expect from me, Matt? Are your feelings hurt because I wouldn't drop everything and dash off to New Orleans this weekend? Is that it?"

"Partly."

"You're going to have to be clearer than that. Whatever it is you're dancing around with this gallery business and assigning 'fault,' I wish you'd just spell it out. I thought we agreed to no games."

Matt looked uncomfortable as he rubbed a hand across the back of his neck. The play of muscle under skin distracted her momentarily, but the loud exhale brought her focus back.

"You want honesty? Fine, I'll be honest. I understand we both went into this with no expectations, but that was before we got to know each other. There's something more between us than just sex—I'm not entirely sure how to describe it—but I think it's worth exploring. I know you feel it, too. Every time I try to move closer, though, you pull away."

Her heart stopped beating momentarily, then came back with a hard thud against her chest. "We've only known each other for that week and a few e-mails."

"Everything has to start somewhere, El."

"But this has nowhere to go," she whispered.

"I think it does. You just have to give it a chance."

Oh, rubbish. "And then what? You live in Atlanta."

"So? We work around that."

"How exactly?"

"Well…"

Matt's well of ready responses finally ran dry. She snorted before she could stop herself. "That's what I thought."

It was his turn to get frustrated, and the heat returned to his voice. "That's what I mean, El," he snapped. "Just because there's not a clear plan right now, that doesn't mean it isn't workable. You have to take a chance some-times. You jump in and make it work."

"I just started a job here. I'm renovating a house. Neither of which will benefit from me running up the roads every weekend."

Matt's eyes widened in disbelief. "A job and a house? *That's* your argument?"

"My job and my house are what I can count on. I can't jeopardize my future on some slim possibility that something might work out between us someday." What on earth did he expect?

"There are other jobs, other houses."

Understanding crept in. "I see. Would those 'other jobs' or 'other houses' possibly be in Atlanta?"

"Maybe. You never know."

"Let's flip this around. I don't see you blithely disregarding your place in your firm. There are other places to practice law, you know."

She could tell she'd made him very uncomfortable this time.

"That's different."

"How?" She took a deep breath in the hopes it would calm her enough to keep her from doing something she might regret. Like making him a permanent soprano. Instead it just seemed to fuel her anger more, and her temper broke loose. "You know, you're right. I am pretty smart, and I can figure this out. Here's how I see it. You see this whole possibility of an 'us,' but I'd lay money this 'us' is in Atlanta, with you still plugging away at making partner. *Nothing* would change for you—hell, you'd have it all."

"Ella—"

She held up a hand to stop him. "Oh, no, I'm just getting started here. It's all becoming so clear. Let's just pretend this 'us' actually happened. Even if I could find a job half as good as the one at SoftWerx, I'd be mostly by myself as you're at work twelve freaking hours a day. Until you decide it's time to give your mom more grandkids, of course, and then I'd have to quit in order to raise them. Or—" Matt wasn't quite meeting her eyes now; she was hitting close to the bone, it seemed "—better yet, maybe until then I could 'live the dream' and paint full-time. Maybe I'd even sell a few and make just enough to feed the cat."

"You're jumping way ahead, Ella, and you know, there *is* a positive spin possible on your scenario."

Matt didn't get it, and she'd go insane trying to explain it to him. "I don't have the luxury of just jumping in and seeing what happens. I don't have a family to fall back on if I go off chasing rainbows and it all goes to hell. All I have is me."

"With that attitude, you'll never have anything more."

"Oh, shut up. I didn't ask you for your opinion or your validation of how *I* want to live *my* life. I didn't sign on to have you second-guess the choices I make. I just wanted to get laid."

Matt pulled back visibly and the harshness of what she'd said registered through the red haze.

"Well, I'm glad I could oblige you on that, at least."

She couldn't think of a response.

Matt took a deep breath, and she held her own, hoping he'd come up with a way to bridge the moat she'd just dug with her temper.

Instead, he shrugged. "It seems like I made a mistake coming here. Several, in fact. Now that everything's clear, and you got the lay you wanted, I'm going to go."

As Matt disappeared into the bedroom, Ella couldn't get her legs to move and words escaped her. Her tirade had shocked her; she certainly hadn't meant for all that to come pouring out.

Matt reappeared fully dressed and carrying his overnight bag. His shoes were untied, she noticed. *Can I blame him for wanting to get the hell out of here as fast as possible?*

"It's been fun, Ella. I'm sorry it worked out like this."

Say something! Don't just let him leave like this.

"Me, too." *That's it. Quit while you're ahead. It's better to end it now.*

"Bye."

"Bye. Drive carefully."

And he was gone.

Just like that.

She took a deep breath and reminded herself it wasn't the first time she'd watched a man beat a fast path for the door. Most of the time she was hurrying them along.

But it had never felt like this.

Instead of the weight lifting off her shoulders because her problem was solved, it seemed to be pressing her down with a force that nearly buckled her knees.

Ella stepped back out on the porch and picked up the quilt from where it landed during her grand exit. Wrapping it around her shoulders, she stared at the empty hammock. It seemed like an eternity had passed since she'd been swinging gently in it, wrapped happily around Matt. Realistically, it hadn't been long at all.

It only takes a minute for everything to change. But she

knew that already from past experience. That's why she planned ahead, covered the possibilities. Too bad she hadn't devised a contingency clause for dealing with Matt.

It was better this way, even if it sucked at the moment. It never should have gone this far in the first place. In the long run, she'd be glad she ended it with Matt now instead of waiting until they were both more deeply involved. Not exactly the most graceful way to extricate herself from a confusing situation, but she wasn't getting points for execution.

It's for the best. She'd been fooling herself, thinking she could dance around the edges with Matt and still come out on top. Her eyes burned and she turned her face into the breeze to cool them.

Now she could get on with her life. She had contractors coming Monday and enough work to keep her busy for a good long while. She'd finally get settled in, and by the New Year, she'd be back on track.

No harm, no foul, she reminded herself. *No one's feelings to get hurt.*

Funny, that's not how it felt at the moment.

Matt made it all the way to the highway before he realized he didn't actually have anywhere to go. When he'd made plans last week, he'd worked on the assumption he'd be at Ella's until tomorrow afternoon. He'd even booked his return flight out of Pensacola so as not to have to make the drive all the way back to New Orleans—plans made to maximize Ella time. It never occurred to him she wouldn't want to see him or that he'd end up out the door at eight on a Saturday night.

What was that saying? "The best-laid plans of mice and men go oft awry." *Awry* was the understatement of the year.

I shouldn't have fought with her. Something about Ella, though, brought out extremes in his normally even keel. The mental replay had him groaning. Walking out in a huff had just been juvenile. He'd pay for those dramatics with a night alone in an airport hotel.

He paused at the junction of the 292 and debated calling her. Maybe he should apologize. He'd come on a bit hard, pushed her too much. Maybe it wasn't too late to work this out.

"I just wanted to get laid." In retrospect, she'd been clear about that from the start. She'd all but spelled it out to him. Only his ego thought the rules had changed, but he'd been set straight tonight.

Yesterday he would have said he knew Ella pretty well. Obviously, he didn't. He should have listened when she tried to end it before.

A honk pulled him back to reality, and a glance in his rearview mirror showed a line of cars backing up behind him.

With a sigh, he turned east toward Pensacola.

CHAPTER NINE

"ARE you ever going to tell me what's eating you, or do I have to go on pretending I don't notice anything wrong?" Melanie punctuated her question with a dramatic sigh.

Ella balanced the phone on her shoulder and leaned back against the headboard. With a good portion of her living areas in various stages of construction, her bedroom was one of the few places in her house not currently in pieces. From her bed, she still had a view of the ocean out over the side porch—an unobstructed view, now that she'd taken down the hammock. The temperatures had dropped too low to sit outside after the sun went down, so she didn't have much reason to be out there until spring arrived. Maybe she'd buy a new hammock then. Or maybe some kind of chaise instead.

Definitely a chaise. Hammocks were nothing but trouble.

"What makes you think there's something wrong?"

"Hel-*lo* this is me you're talking to. Your voice

sounds funny, you're less talkative than usual—even your e-mails are blue-tinged. Something's been bugging you for a over a week now, and I'm driving myself crazy worrying about it."

Mel's question put her in a bad position. She could lie or make excuses for her mood, but there was a ninety-eight-percent chance Mel would see it for what it was. Obviously, the pretend-everything-is-just-fine route wasn't working, so continuing to plod along there would be a waste of time. Either of those options would also keep Mel on high worry alert, and everyone suffered when Mel worried.

Too bad the truth wasn't an option.

"I think it's just the settling-in blues. Work is taking more out of me than I planned, and the work on the house is slow going. You know what a control freak I am. All the upheaval is just getting to me. I'm a little homesick, as well."

"I can have a moving truck at your house tomorrow."

That brought a laugh. Even funnier was that Mel was dead serious. If she listened closely, she'd probably hear the yellow pages rustling as Mel looked up moving companies.

"I'm not kidding, El. There's the cutest vacant apartment just a block from here that would be perfect for you. Plus, I ran into Abe Morris the other day at the market. He said he'd kill to have you back. He mentioned a raise and a possible promotion."

"Which, technically, I should have gotten two years

ago. He's just sore he has to actually work these days instead of hiding in his office playing computer games. You know he keeps e-mailing me with questions, right? Thanks, but I think I'm good where I am."

"You could have fooled me. You sound miserable."

She tried for a light tone. "I'm fine, Mel. Seriously."

"Whatever it is, you can tell me."

"I know. And if there was anything to tell, I would." She salved her guilty conscience with the fact there wasn't anything to tell now. Nothing Melanie could do to help, either. "Stop worrying. When I get there Wednesday, you'll be able to see for yourself that I'm fine."

"I'll meet you at the airport. And Mom is making sweet potatoes just for you."

"It wouldn't be Thanksgiving without them."

Slipping out from under Mel's microscope, Ella breathed a sigh of relief. After a few more minutes, she was able to get off the phone and halt the line of questioning.

She doubted Mel believed her story, but it would buy her a little more time. Not that she had much available. She had four days to pull it together before she flew to Chicago to spend Thanksgiving with Mel and her family. If Mel was picking up on her misery so easily now, she was in trouble the second she stepped off the plane.

Thirteen days. Thirteen days since Matt left. No phone calls. No e-mails. Nothing. It was as if they'd never met.

Oh, but they had. And the ache that set up camp in her chest was a constant reminder.

She'd gotten used to him too quickly. She should've

listened to the little voice in her head and not let herself get so close. She should have ended it completely and in no uncertain terms before she ever left Chicago. She should've turned down his offer of a fling. Hell, she never should've slept with him in the first place.

Then she wouldn't be in love with him now.

It'd taken four days of misery and heartache for her to admit that to herself. How and when she'd fallen for him was a mystery, but she was inexplicably in love with the infuriating man. Which was exactly what she'd wanted to avoid.

She didn't do well in relationships. Never had. It was too difficult when they reached the end, so she learned to not start anything she wouldn't be able to get out of easily. Matt wasn't content with just crawling into her bed. Oh, no, he hadn't stopped until he'd crawled into her head and heart as well.

What she'd thought was just hormonal infatuation was proving to be something much more, and now it was eating her alive. If the pain was all she had to deal with, she'd be okay. She'd dealt with worse. But the sinking feeling of regret—of a loss she couldn't quite put her finger on—was the worst part.

She didn't like the regrets.

A niggling voice in the back of her mind whispered she'd really screwed up this time. That Matt was worth hanging on to, even if it would be difficult—in every way imaginable—to do so.

She returned the phone to its cradle and pulled her

paint-splattered shirt over her head, covering her to her knees. Although she tried not to, her eyes kept wandering to the chair across from the bed.

A gray sweatshirt sporting PENN in big letters lay folded there. She'd found it the day after Matt left, turned inside out from a hasty removal and accidentally kicked halfway under the bed. Even now she could picture the look on Matt's face as he'd pulled it over his head and let it fall.

How to return it was a mystery. She couldn't pass it off to Mel or Brian to return without garnering the third degree. She didn't have his home address—and it wasn't listed, she had checked—and sending forgotten clothing to his office screamed bad taste.

The faint smell of Matt's aftershave still clung to it. Simply folding the sweatshirt had brought tears to her eyes. She hadn't touched it since then. Eventually she'd have to.

Later, after the rawness eases a bit.

She padded barefoot to the other room, where her brushes and palette were waiting, and perched on the battered stool. Squinting critically at the canvas, she decided it wasn't that bad. Working with the oils was more difficult, but all and all, it was turning into a cathartic experience. Painting allowed the hours to pass without much thought on her part. It was all about focus, and it kept her mind from wandering away from the canvas to painful, regret-filled places.

She took a deep breath, the pain in her chest expanding with her lungs. She focused on breathing out slowly, clearing her mind and reminding herself that this, too, would pass.

It had to.

"These need your signature, these are for your reviewing pleasure, and this is your travel itinerary." Matt's assistant tilted her head as she handed over the last item. "You're going home for Thanksgiving? In five years, I've never known you to go away for the holidays."

Matt took the printout and laid it aside. "Yeah, well, normally I don't. But I kind of promised to this year."

Debbie smiled. "I know your mother will be happy." She headed for her desk in the outer office. "Don't forget a coat," she tossed over her shoulder. "The weather forecast for Chicago is pretty chilly."

With his luck, they'd get an early snow. If he hadn't already told his mother he'd be there, he'd spend the long weekend on the golf course and save himself the hassle. But after promising Ella last month, he'd told his mother to save him a seat at the adults' table. Now he was stuck.

Ella. He had to stop thinking about her. She'd made herself and her feelings pretty clear, and the stunning silence from her left no room for misunderstanding.

Ella's silence—along with the massive workload awaiting his return—had actually helped. The distance helped increase his clarity, and he was able to see his infatuation for what it was. He'd been crazy to even consider it might be something more than that. Ella was funny, smart, beautiful and good in bed, and he'd just gotten carried away.

There was a first time for everything. Thank God he'd gotten it under control. He should be thanking her for ending it before it went any further and someone got hurt.

His eyes landed on his itinerary again. Most likely, Ella would be in for the holiday, as well. If so, she'd be staying with Melanie and Brian. It's not as though Ella had other family to go see for the holiday. There was a very good chance he'd see her.

His body reacted instantly, hardening at the thought of her. The rational part of his big brain might be clear on the realities of the situation, but his little brain wasn't there yet. It was annoying as hell.

But it wouldn't be a problem. They were adults. They'd hooked up, but now it was over. The limited contact they might have to have wouldn't be an issue.

No problem at all.

CHAPTER TEN

THE nightmare of air travel the day before Thanksgiving wasn't unexpected, but sharing a row for three hours with the woman who had marinated herself in a cloying gardenia scent brought on a full-fledged allergy attack. By the time she landed in Chicago, Ella's nose was running, her eyes were streaming and a migraine was splitting her head apart. Simply getting to clean air hadn't been enough; the scent clung to her clothes and hair, feeding the attack until she got to Melanie's and headed straight for the shower.

Liberal doses of antihistamines and what sleep she could manage with her head pounding had helped some, but she woke Thursday morning still sneezing and coughing and generally feeling like death warmed over.

But there was a silver lining. Mel had something concrete to fuss over instead of only vague suspicions, and any quietness on Ella's part could be chalked up to the allergy attack. Hacking and blowing her way though Thanksgiving lunch with Mel's entire family seemed a small price to pay for the reprieve from Mel's prying questions.

Her misery also allowed her to decline Brian's invitation to go to his family's for dinner that night. She'd been considering going, just for Mel's sake, until Matt called Brian's cell and Brian extended the same invitation to him.

So Matt had made good on his offhand promise to come home for Thanksgiving. He was *here*. The last thing she needed was to intentionally put herself in close proximity to him. Hell, being in the same town felt a little too close for comfort.

Any progress she'd made in the past few days in the "getting over Matt" department receded at the thought of actually seeing him. No way she was ready for that. No, no, no.

Thankfully, her next coughing fit had been enough to allow her to beg off, and instead she was dropped at Melanie's apartment to rest.

"Are you sure you don't want me to call the doctor?"

"On Thanksgiving? I'd have to be half-dead to agree. I've got good medicine, so I'm going to have a cup of tea and crawl under the covers for a while. I'll be fine. Go. Have fun."

Mel wasn't totally convinced, but eventually she left. Ella made tea in Mel's ugly china cups and snuggled down on the sofa to watch TV and doze.

When the phone rang a while later, she let the machine pick it up.

"It's Matt."

Ella sat straight up on the couch at the sound of his voice, the hazy medicinal fog clearing immediately from the shot of adrenaline in her veins.

"When Brian starts looking for his cell, I have it. It ended up in my coat pocket somehow. Unless you need it, I'll bring it with me tomorrow when I come. Oh, and tell Mel I'm bringing Kelly with me."

Seventeen emotions slammed into her at once, all of them jockeying for attention. Matt. *Tomorrow?* There's a Kelly? She barely had time to catch her breath, much less sort through any of them, before she heard a key in the lock.

Breathe in; breathe out. Act naturally. "Hey, y'all."

"El! I thought you'd be asleep for sure. Are you feeling okay?" Mel jumped straight into concern mode.

"A nap helped." Trying to sound casual, she indicated the answering machine and its blinking light. "Um, Matt called. He said he got Brian's cell phone by mistake."

Brian patted his coat pocket. "I hadn't even noticed."

"He, um, also said something about bringing some-one tomorrow."

Brian merely nodded.

Well, that was unhelpful.

Melanie fussed about, fluffing her pillow and of-fering to make more tea.

Time for a direct approach. "So what's happening tomorrow?"

"Don't you know?" The look of confusion on

Melanie's face seemed genuine. "We're hosting the post-turkey football fest this year. It should be fun. I'm glad you're feeling better—I'd hate for you to be miserable all day."

A mild case of panic set in. On top of everything else roiling around inside her, she might throw up. Brian chose that moment to replay Matt's message, and the sound of his voice intensified the nausea. So much for "feeling better." She cleared her throat. "Is that what Matt's talking about? Coming here tomorrow?"

Mel nodded and Ella's stomach knotted. "I wonder who this Kelly is, though."

Yeah, me, too, damn it. Jealousy spiked through her. She really just needed to go lie down in the other room.

"Ross Kelly's a guy we used to go to school with. He's in Florida now, probably not too far from you, Ella. He's a computer geek, too, but more hardware, I think. You two should have lots to talk about."

She wanted to smack herself for the relief that washed over her due to a male Kelly.

Mel's eyes lit up. "Is he cute?"

Brian shrugged. "I have no idea. He's Kelly."

Oh, no. She knew that look. "No, Mel. I'm not interested, and you're not allowed to matchmake anymore."

"You're never going to forgive me for the Donovan fiasco, are you? That was years ago." Melanie pouted.

Ella rubbed her temples. The bed beckoned. She needed quiet to sort through the mess in her head, and the thought of being set up with anyone—particularly a friend of Matt's—had her choking back hysterical laughter.

She was able to cover it with a coughing fit that had Mel clucking over her in sympathy and hustling her off to bed in the guest room. Mentally she thanked her seatmate for the stench yesterday. Illness of any sort had never been so handy before.

She collapsed in the bed with a dramatic sigh that wasn't the least bit faked. Melanie fussed over her until she wanted to scream, but finally she was alone. The crashing emotions and surges of adrenaline had taken their toll on her, and her head started to pound again.

Tomorrow. Matt would be *here,* in this very apartment, tomorrow. She'd have to face him, and she wasn't sure if she could. What on earth would she say? Plus, she wasn't exactly at her best right now—emotionally *or* physically—and she was pretty sure she looked like hell on toast.

Maybe she could pretend to have a relapse and just spend the entire day in the bed. That would save her a lot of pain and heartache.

This trip is turning into a nightmare.

The sleep she desperately needed eluded her. She lay awake, listening to the sounds of Brian and Melanie getting ready for bed and the silence that followed. No matter what she did, her thoughts kept returning to Matt.

She missed him.

Tell him, the little voice in her head whispered, and

her heartbeat accelerated at the thought. *What's the worst that could happen?*

"I could make an even bigger fool of myself," she mumbled into her pillow.

But it was an idea worth further thought. Maybe, just maybe, she might have the opportunity to say something—*what* exactly she wasn't sure yet. It would depend on how he acted tomorrow—she'd have to wait and see.

On second thought, that "relapse" didn't sound like such a bad idea. It would give her a great reason to avoid contact with Matt until she had a chance to judge his behavior.

And, if Matt seemed like he might still be interested, well, then, she could apologize for being such a witch and see if the damage she'd caused was beyond repair.

It was worth a shot, right? Or was she better off just letting the whole thing go?

She groaned and punched the pillow into a more comfortable shape. Ella stared at the ceiling and wondered how many more sleepless nights Matt would bring.

He'd known good and well that Ella would be here today. He'd come anyway, telling himself that it was no big deal. That they were both adults who could be polite acquaintances after they'd both moved on after a mutually good time. That Ella was just another woman from his past—even if it was a fairly recent past. That he was here to see his friends and watch the game.

He'd been partly right. Ella seemed to have the "no

big deal" attitude down pat. She hadn't even blinked when he walked in.

That stung.

Her polite "Good to see you again" had been cool and cordial, and she'd made polite small talk for the requisite two minutes before moving away to watch one of the three TVs Brian had set up in various parts of the apartment. She'd been uncharacteristically quiet and slightly withdrawn all afternoon, claiming she didn't feel all that great. As she supposedly didn't know him any more than she knew any of Brian's friends—and some of them were still holding a grudge from the wedding—no one could accuse her of being rude even though she was, for the most part, pretending he wasn't there.

But he was well aware of her presence. His entire body was on high alert just from the proximity, and his attention kept wandering from the game.

She shouldn't be out here trying to be sociable if she doesn't feel well. She should be in bed. He'd be happy to join her there.

"She's not contagious or anything."

He looked up to see Brian holding another beer out to him. "What?"

"Ella. She sounds sick, but she's not spreading germs to all of us. Beer?"

"Thanks." As he took the bottle, he heard another round of coughing. Since Brian broached the topic, it seemed safe to comment. "What's wrong with her?"

"Bad allergy attack. Some woman on the plane had

enough perfume on to drown an elephant, and that set her off. Nasty smell—and so strong I had to air out the car after just bringing Ella here."

Must've been gardenias. She'd mentioned an allergy once...

Brian regained his attention by pointing at the table behind him, groaning under the weight of the food. "We kept her away from the food, just in case, so it's safe to eat."

"Did you call a caterer? Ella says Mel can barely boil water." He didn't realize the implications of his words until Brian paused, his beer bottle halfway to his mouth. *Aw, damn.*

"'Ella says?' I thought you two were getting mighty chatty at the wedding. Although I find it interesting Ella would bad-mouth Mel's cooking at her own wedding." Brian's eyebrow went up in challenge.

Ella's desire to keep everything down low was coming back to haunt him. Great. Silence was the safest course.

Brian shrugged. "Hooking up with the maid of honor is a cliché, but Ella's not a bad choice. *If* you did, of course. There's little evidence to go on, Counselor."

Except what comes out of my own big mouth. "Does Melanie think...?"

"Good God, no. Mel doesn't think anything. You'd know if she did. She'd be all over both of you if she had the smallest suspicion."

Ella had given him a similar warning. Good thing they'd been discreet or today would be even more awkward. Not that it matters, he reminded himself. He and Ella were ancient history.

Brian leaned in and lowered his voice. "But do me a favor. Whatever did or did not happen between you two, don't mess Ella around. I do *not* want Ella unhappy."

Matt tried to keep his tone light, but Brian's protective stance rankled him. "Since when are you the champion of all womankind? Channeling Sir Galahad these days?"

"Hardly. Ella can hold her own with the likes of you. My interest is completely self-serving."

"I'm not following you."

"Then listen carefully. If you make Ella unhappy, *my* life will become a living hell. Melanie will land on *you* with both feet, but I'm the one who has to live with her and listen to it. Tread carefully where Ella's concerned."

At least Brian was clear. Matt nodded. "Duly noted, but an unnecessary warning. There's nothing going on, so Mel has no reason to jump on either of us."

"Glad to hear it."

Melanie chose that moment to join them. Brian reached up and pulled her into his lap, where she settled with a comfortable smile. "Glad you could make it today, Matt. I half expected your mother not to let you out of her sight."

"Even my mother tires of me eventually."

"I can't imagine why." She punctuated the statement with a smile, but then cleared her throat and pinned him with a sharp stare. "But enough small talk. I have serious matters to deal with, and you can provide me with the information I need."

"If you're in trouble with the law, Mel, I won't be of much help," he teased. "I don't handle criminal cases."

She snorted. "I'm on the right side of the law, so no worries there. It's Ella."

Matt nearly choked on his beer, but caught himself in time and swallowed painfully instead. "Ella?"

"I'm worried about her being so far away, and I'm afraid she's going to be lonely."

It would be of her own making. "And?"

"*And,* I'm thinking Ross Kelly might be a good person to hook her up with."

Brian interrupted. "Don't meddle, Mel," he warned.

Jealousy crawled over him. Melanie wanted to fix Ella up with one of his friends? Oh, the irony.

"I'll meddle if I want. El is my business, so butt out." She held up a hand to silence her husband and turned her attention back to Matt. "He's cute, and he seems nice enough, but I need more information. What's he like? Is he seeing anyone? You've met El—do you think they might hit it off?"

At least he could answer truthfully. "I honestly don't know. Kelly's not a bad guy, but I'm not privy to his personal life, and I don't know what Ella's looking for in a guy." *That* was the understatement of the year.

Melanie sighed. "Men are so unhelpful. You've known him since high school and that's the best you can do?"

Matt shrugged as Brian nodded.

"Then it's time for reconnaissance. Come on." Melanie stood and tugged Brian to his feet. "I'd like to get to know your friend."

Brian protested as Melanie dragged him away. Under other circumstances, Matt would have found the situation amusing, but considering Melanie's mission, it wasn't remotely funny. He nursed his beer and pretended to watch the game. His football team was losing by a stunning margin, but he couldn't dredge up much interest.

The crowd in the room grew as other games ended and everyone migrated to watch the final quarter of the big game on the big-screen TV. After raising eyebrows when he couldn't answer questions about what happened earlier in the game—even though he'd been staring at the screen intently the entire time—Matt went to the kitchen under the guise of needing another beer.

He found Ella instead.

"Hey."

She jumped at the sound of his voice, nearly dropping the plastic cup she held. Soda splashed over her hand onto the counter. "Oops."

"Didn't mean to startle you."

Ella shrugged as she wiped the counter and dried her hands. "It's not your fault. I didn't hear you come in." She laughed nervously. "I'm on a lot of antihistamines and a bit out of it."

"But they must be working. You're looking much better than you did earlier." In reality she looked uncomfortable and slightly wary.

And so good it took everything he had not to reach for her.

Ella wasn't meeting his eyes. She took her time folding the towel in her hands and smiled weakly. "It takes a while to work its way out of my system, but I'm on the mend."

"Gardenias?"

Her eyes snapped up to meet his. "Yeah. I can't believe you remember that."

"Of course."

Ella cleared her throat and looked away again, fidgeting with the towel, her cup and finally her belt. Their stilted conversation was so different from what they'd had before—even at the very beginning, they'd never had the awkward what-to-say-now problem. The gaping silence that came now, though, was even worse. But he didn't want to cut his losses and walk out of the room. Retreat wasn't an option. Not when it was his first—and possibly only—chance to talk to Ella privately. The problem was what to say next. A list of questions unfolded in his head, but none seemed appropriate in this situation. He settled on the lame but safe, "How've you been?"

Ella lifted her chin and plastered a fake smile on her face. "Good. Staying busy with work and the renovations. How about you?"

"Good." More silence followed their pitiful attempt at conversation.

Ella broke the stalemate first this time. "I see you followed though on your promise to come home for Thanksgiving. Your mom must be very pleased."

"She is. I haven't told her anything about Christmas yet, though. The excitement might be too much for her to handle. I guess Melanie was also glad to have you back for the weekend."

"Except for the sneezing part, she was." Ella took a deep breath and he could see her forcing herself to relax. She leaned a hip against the counter and shoved her hands into her pockets. "Matt, I want…" She trailed off and broke eye contact again.

"You want what?" He knew her well enough to know that she was screwing up the courage to say whatever it was she wanted to say, but he didn't want her to lose her nerve before she did. Out if habit he started to reach for her, but caught himself in time. "Come on, El. I think we're past the beat-around-the-bush stage."

She nodded. "I wanted to apologize. For the way things ended."

Ended. Past tense. *Right.* They were over and Ella had moved on. Hell, Melanie was lining up the next contestant right this second. That shouldn't bother him, but it did. "It wasn't my best moment, either. I'll accept your apology if you'll accept mine."

Her smile hit like a dagger to his chest. "Done. And I'm so glad. I'd hate it if after everything, we ended up as enemies because of my temper."

But we're not ending up as friends, either. "Yeah," he managed to bite out.

"I handled this whole thing badly. I wish…"

Couldn't she just let it drop? He was trying to respect

her wishes here, but she wasn't making it easy to do so. "No. You were right—"

She touched him then, her hand landing on his arm like a hot coal, the muscles underneath tensing in response. "Matt, what I'm trying to say is that…"

"Ella? Are you in here?" Melanie pushed open the kitchen door, and Ella jumped and backed away. The hand that was already reaching for her dropped to his side. "And you, too, Matt? Folks were wondering where you disappeared to."

Ella cleared her throat. "We just got to talking."

"Well, that's nice." Melanie looked at him strangely, then turned her attention back to Ella. "I'm sorry to interrupt, but I want you to come meet Ross Kelly."

"But I met him earlier, Mel."

"Yes, but I've had a chance to talk to him, and I think you two should get to know each other better. You have tons in common."

What Melanie lacked in subtlety, she made up for in determination, and Ella rolled her eyes as she tried to decline. Again, the situation was almost amusing. *Almost.*

"Mel, I'm in the middle of a conversation here. Can you give me a minute, at least?"

Melanie took a deep breath to argue, and Ella looked ready to snap. He gave her—and himself—an escape route. "It's okay. Go with Mel. I think we've covered everything we need to."

Obviously pleased she was going to get her way, Melanie reached for Ella's hand. "Come on. I need to get dinner put together, and you shouldn't be in here sneezing all over everything. You can talk to Ross while I get things ready. Matt, you can help Brian grill the burgers."

That got his attention. "Grill? It's only forty degrees outside."

"The fire will keep you warm. Come *on,* Ella."

Ella sent a pleading look over her shoulder as Melanie dragged her from the room. He might not like it, but there wasn't anything he could do about it. She'd said her piece and really—as much as it might kill him to admit it—Ella wasn't his business anymore.

"So? What did you think of Ross?"

Most of the crowd was long gone. Only a hardy few of Brian's friends, including Matt, still camped out in the living room. Pronounced well enough to help clean up and drafted into kitchen duty, Ella had been expecting Mel's question as she scraped plates and loaded the dishwasher. Mel was too predictable. Not even five minutes alone before starting in on her. "He seems nice enough."

"That's it? Nice enough? El, he's practically perfect for you, and I can tell by the way he watched you at dinner that he's very interested."

Too interested. Any more so and he'd have been in her lap. And Matt, damn him, hadn't even looked at her once the whole meal. She sat right across from him for an entire meal, and he said exactly four words to her: "Please pass the salt." They'd bumped feet under the table a few times—only once was on purpose—and he'd moved away as if she was on fire. She'd like to think it was because of Ross, but the knot in her stomach told her it was more likely the fact that Matt had put her out of his mind. "Yeah, well…"

"Please tell me you gave him your phone number, at least. E-mail address? Something?"

"E-mail."

Melanie's eyes crinkled as she smiled. "Good."

"Don't get all excited. I'm not that interested in him."

"Well, I don't think you should be blowing off pos-sibilities considering you and Matt seem to be in a stalemate."

The plate she was holding clattered into the sink. "Excuse me?"

"Good Lord, do you think I'm stupid? Or just blind?" Mel arched an eyebrow at her. "You've been staring at him all day like he's covered in chocolate and you'd like a taste."

The mental image slammed into her, nearly causing her knees to buckle in lust.

Mel kept talking. "And Matt. I've never seen some-one try so hard to pretend he's not aware someone exists. The boy's not a good actor, that's for sure. Are you going to tell me what all of this is about?"

"Well…I…um…" So much for keeping the whole thing quiet and off Melanie's radar. She felt light-headed and hoped it was just the medicine.

Melanie crossed her arms and leaned a hip against

the counter. "Well, *that's* enlightening. Maybe I should go talk to Matt, hmm?"

"Mel, no!"

Melanie took hold of her elbow and led her to the small breakfast table. She pushed Ella into a chair, then sat opposite her. "Spill it."

Easier said than done. "It's complicated."

"You two hooked up after the wedding, didn't you? I'd heard about 'some guy' who'd been at the apartment with you while I was gone, but I didn't piece together that it was Matt." Mel's voice softened and dropped a notch. "What's going on?"

Ella rested her chin on her hands. "We went to dinner the next night, and, *yes,*" she added at Melanie's knowing grin, "we hooked up. He stayed with me until I left for home."

Melanie's eyebrows disappeared into her hairline. "The *whole* week? Oh, my," she sighed, as a dreamy look crossed her face. "Don't tell Brian, but I'm a teeny bit jealous. Those shoulders…"

Ella joined her in the sigh. "Trust me, I know."

"And…"

"And that was supposed to be it. Just a fling. No strings. No commitments. Nothing messy." She paused, and when she was able to speak again, her voice was barely above a pitiful-sounding whisper. "Except that it got messy."

"Oh, *El.* Tell me you didn't—"

"I did." She rubbed her eyes as Mel tsked. "I got comfortable, then Matt got *too* comfortable, and he moved in a little too fast. He started to push—"

"And you pushed back," Mel finished for her.

"Yeah."

"El, we've talked about this. You've *got* to get past this emotional abstinence thing. There are a lot of great guys out there—if you'll just give one a chance."

"I know. And I even tried to. With Matt, I mean. But then he was at the house and he kept pushing me about—"

Melanie held up a hand. "Wait. Matt was at your house? In Alabama? *When?*"

Oops. Maybe that was too much information. "Two weeks ago. He'd been in New Orleans for business and drove over for the weekend."

"You've been hooked up with Matt for over a month and you never told me?" Mel said in a near shout.

"Shh. Tell the world, why don't you?" Ella paused to listen, but the noise level from the other room hadn't changed. "We weren't hooked up. We were just friends. Kinda," she added as an afterthought. "Then Matt started hinting about possibilities and I panicked. We didn't exactly part on the best of terms."

"And now?"

She shrugged. "Matt's over it. Out of sight, out of mind, I guess. I haven't talked to him in two weeks, and whatever attraction he had to me must have passed." Her voice cracked a little. "Like you said, he pretty much avoided me all day. And earlier, when we were talking, he seemed to be happy to put the whole thing to rest."

"What about you?"

Ella chewed her bottom lip as she thought about it. *No sense in lying.* "I'll get there."

Melanie's eyes widened. "You mean…?"

"Yeah." Tears burned in the corners of her eyes and she swiped at them.

"So that's what's been eating you lately."

She nodded, and a short bitter laugh escaped. "Serves me right, doesn't it? I've been pushing people away for so long, now it's my turn to see how it feels. Matt seemed safe, and I let my guard down. I didn't mean to fall in love with him."

"You're *in love* with him? Oh my God, Ella. I didn't realize it had gone *that* far." Mel's fingers reached out to wipe the tears off Ella's cheekbones before fluffing the hair around her face. "There. Your eyes are still a little red, but that's okay. Wait here. I'll keep everyone out after I send Matt in."

Mel stood and Ella grabbed her hand. "No! Don't you dare send Matt in here. We're done. I apologized for the way things ended, and Matt's okay with that."

"But you need to tell him how you feel."

Ella massaged her temples. Mel was such a romantic. "This isn't some movie, Mel. I told you, Matt's over it. Case closed."

"Case closed, like hell! If you ask me—"

"I didn't." She used the sternest voice she had. "In

fact, I'm telling you to butt out. We are adults, and we can handle this like adults. In fact," she continued, "it's handled already. It's not like I'll have to see him all that often or anything, so it's a done deal."

"Ella…" Melanie cajoled.

"Melanie…" she warned.

Mel closed her eyes and shook her head. "Fine. Whatever. You're the most stubborn person I've ever met."

Magnanimous in her victory and safe from Mel's meddling, she reached out to pat her hand. "Would it make you feel better if I promised to reply to Ross's e-mail—if he sends me one, of course."

Normally that promise would satisfy Mel, so the slight grimace crossing her face surprised Ella. "Maybe Ross isn't the best choice for you right now."

Talk about a turnaround. "Why not?"

"He's a friend of Matt's and that would be uncomfortable even if you and Matt had ended gracefully. With things like they are…well, you're rebounding, and that's really not good for you or Ross."

"I am not rebounding!"

"The view from here says differently."

"Then you need glasses. Yes, I got in over my head, and my heart ended up a little bruised, but I'm not—"

"Rebounding?" Melanie mocked.

"Oh, be quiet."

Melanie rolled her eyes and sighed, and they sat there in silence for a moment. Oddly enough, the skirmish with Mel had made her feel a little better.

Mel broke the silence first. "I'll tell you what. Include dinner and a fair chance for Ross, and I'll keep my mouth shut."

"And you'll quit accusing me of rebounding?"

"Only if you're careful—for both your sakes."

"Done." Ella extended her hand.

Melanie shook on it, and her face softened. "You know I just want you to be happy, right?"

"Yeah, I know. And I love you for it. I have a few more years before I have to give up and get a bunch of cats to keep me company, though, so don't panic just yet. Okay?"

"Okay."

Melanie kept giving her strange looks as they finished tidying the kitchen, but she kept the topics neutral without any mention of Matt—or any other man, thank goodness.

Melanie planned to join the others for a movie, but Ella pleaded fatigue. She stopped off in the living room on her way to the bedroom for courtesy's sake, only for Matt to all but ignore her again. It was more than she could take, and she retreated to the safety of the guest room.

She couldn't blame Matt. She'd treated him badly, and his behavior was understandable. It wasn't his fault she had regrets. She'd come so close—*too* close—to spilling her guts to him in the kitchen earlier, and now she was glad she hadn't. She'd been right all along. Now that they weren't in each other's pockets, Matt had moved on.

And as much as it hurt her, she had no choice but to do the same.

CHAPTER ELEVEN

HE WASN'T a morning-jog kind of person, but this was the third time this week he'd seen the sun come up as he pounded six miles on the pavement.

The most erotic dreams—all starring Ella—were disturbing his sleep, and they'd only gotten more explicit since he returned from Chicago on Sunday night. He'd wake up with raging hard-ons and, with zero chance of getting the subject of his nighttime fantasies to act them out, he fell back on the age-old way of releasing tension.

Mind-numbing, sweat-producing, energy-expending exercise.

In the past few weeks, he'd increased his distance by a mile and still decreased his time. He could give Ella and Roscoe a run for their money now—not that he'd have the opportunity.

He was in the best shape of his life.

His breath came in steaming puffs as he stopped at the corner store for a newspaper and a bottle of water.

He'd take a shower, grab some breakfast and be at the driving range by nine.

He took the stairs two at a time to the third floor and fished out his keys as he turned down the hallway toward his apartment. He read the headlines as he walked, so the voice that greeted him as he neared his door caught him by surprise.

"Matt! I was just looking for you. I didn't expect you to be out and about so early on a Saturday morning."

Gillian stepped toward the door as he opened it, and he waved her in. She had a small bag from the neighborhood bakery in her hand.

"Best time to run. What can I do for you?" He tossed the paper and his keys on the counter as he rounded it and headed into the kitchen. "Coffee?"

She shook her head and leaned against the arm of the couch. "I just wanted to thank you. She's great."

"Who's great?"

"Your friend. Ella Mackenzie. Some really good work."

That got his attention. He drained the last of the water in his bottle before he spoke. "Ella?"

"Yeah, I got images from her yesterday. My boss is going to love her—regional, mostly self-taught—the promo is going to write itself." She grinned. "Since I, of course, will be claiming all of the credit for discovering this Outsider talent, I brought you a cookie in thanks." She held out the bag to him.

He took it absently and set it on the counter. "Ella sent you images? Of her paintings?"

"You're a bit slow today, aren't you?" She spoke very slowly, as if he was a dim bulb. "Yes. Ella sent work for evaluation. It is good. I am going to call her. Thank you for sending her my way."

"I'm just surprised she sent anything. She seemed so against the idea when I mentioned it."

"Well, she obviously changed her mind. And thank goodness she did. The gallery is doing a 'New South— New Talent' exhibition in March, and I'm going to offer her space."

Good for Ella. He wasn't sure if he should be proud *of* her or *for* her, but either way he was happy for her. He'd known she had talent with just one look at her art. The feeling of being proven right was a pathetic consolation prize, though.

Gillian stretched and wiggled her fingers, obviously pleased about something. "I'm going to celebrate my fantastic new discovery with the boots I saw at Nordstrom's last week." She watched as he wiped sweat off his neck and wrinkled her nose. "I sincerely hope your next stop is the shower, so I'll leave you to it." Gillian stood. "I can show myself out."

He walked her to the door anyway, unstrapping his iPod holder from his arm as he went.

Gillian was completely out the door when she stopped and said with a grin, "Oh, and let me just say…yowza."

Huh? "Yowza?"

Her grin got bigger. "That one of you—I assume it's you, right?—is smokin' hot."

"I have no idea what you're talking about."

"Honey, if you want to make some cash on the side, I know plenty of people who'd hire you to model."

Was she on drugs? Gillian wasn't making any sense at all. "Hold on a second. First of all, I don't pose for anything. Second—what 'one' are you talking about?"

Gillian's forehead furrowed in confusion. "Ella sent twelve works for me to look at. All of them were landscapes, except for the last one, an oil portrait, which she said wasn't quite finished. When I saw it, I just assumed the man in the painting was you. You said you two were pretty close friends, and it certainly looks like you." She paused, and her eyes widened. "You mean you didn't know?"

He stepped out in the hall and closed the door behind him. "Show me."

Gillian led the way to her apartment—which, while it had the same floor plan as his, definitely showed her more-artistic side, with abstract art lining the walls and eclectic furniture. A black laptop, completely at odds with the riot of color around it, sat on her coffee table.

A few clicks of the mouse and Gillian was in her e-mail account. "She attached them in a PowerPoint presentation. She's a bit of a computer geek, isn't she?" She laughed, but when he didn't join her, she sobered instantly. "Let me scroll through."

Images flashed across the screen. He recognized a few of the paintings as ones he'd seen in her apartment that day. Cityscapes, beachscapes—all showcasing Ella's fascination with the play of light.

"Here it is." Gillian passed him the laptop. "She mentions that it still needs some finishing, but I think it's very captivating. It shows a lot of skill—I mean, just look at the attention to detail. Even the underpainting is…"

Gillian's voice faded to a drone in the background as Ella's bedroom in the Chicago apartment filled the screen. He'd have recognized it anywhere. It was a night scene, the bedroom dark and the area around her bed only faintly illuminated from the streetlight he knew was just outside that window. A square of light and a woman's shadow stretched across the floor from the front of the painting, as if the woman had opened the door between Ella's living room and the bedroom and stood looking in the doorway with the light behind her. That light only touched the edges of the room, but Matt could see where the walls were bare and boxes sat stacked in the dim corners. A T-shirt and a pair of jeans lay on the floor, dropped and forgotten.

But the focal point of the painting was the bed and the man who filled it. Big and broad-shouldered, he was shirtless as he slept on his stomach. Blue-striped sheets tangled around him, exposing one leg from the knee down, and bunched at his waist. He was alone in the bed, one arm thrown over where the shadow woman might have been sleeping previously.

Recognition and realization slammed into him, and the air left his lungs. Ella had painted him. *Him.*

Sleeping in her bed. It was surreal, but the boxes, the bedroom—it was exactly as it had looked weeks ago as he'd helped her pack. That had to be him in the bed. Maybe his shoulders weren't really that broad, but the hair was right. And how many other men spent the night in her apartment while she was packing?

Gillian continued to praise the painting, fully in critic mode now as she pointed out different aspects. "This is very different from her watercolor landscapes, telling me she has great versatility. That sharp contrast between the light and dark you see is called *chiaroscuro,* and Ella has it down pat. I'm going to encourage her to do more oils in the future."

Her finger traced over the screen as she talked, and he was hard-pressed to pay attention to what she was saying—especially since it was *him,* front and center.

Her finger brushed across the man. "That is you, right? I mean, the features aren't clear, but, honey, I recognize those lats and delts from the weight room downstairs." Gillian clicked to the Notes section. "She calls it *Fling.*"

His stomach clenched. Fling. Trust Ella to put a fine point on it. That's exactly what they'd had. But still…

"E-mail this to me."

Gillian drew back. "I can't go forwarding her work around without permission."

"Just send it."

He left Gillian sputtering on her couch and went back to his apartment.

Turning the shower on as hot as it would go, he

stripped and stepped under the spray. Thousands of tiny needles tried to beat the tension from his muscles without success.

Ella had painted him. She hadn't even bothered to mention it to him. He thought back to that weekend-gone-wrong at her house. He'd seen a draped canvas on an easel but hadn't asked about it. He'd had other things on his mind at the time—namely getting her horizontal—and it had disappeared to another room shortly after his arrival. Had that been the painting under the sheet? Not that he had a clue as to how long it would take Ella to paint something like that, but she had to have been working on it for a while to be able to send a photo of it to Gillian—unfinished or not.

Maybe the "finishing" Ella mentioned to Gillian involved adding horns and a devil's tail.

At the same time, it was satisfying to think she'd been affected enough by their time together to even consider painting him—fling or not. Regardless of how it all ended, she hadn't been able to completely dismiss him from her mind.

He turned the water all the way to cold for a minute, then turned it off completely and reached for a towel. This thing with Ella was one giant mess. He'd found the perfect woman. Only she lived in a different state, had a hair-trigger temper and possessed deep-rooted problems where relationships were concerned. Just his luck to fall in love with a woman who wanted nothing to do with him.

His hand stilled, as the reason for that hollow feeling in his stomach became clear with that thought. *He loved Ella.* How or when or even *why*—for God's sake—he didn't know, but it was the only possible explanation.

And it explained so much. Not that he had any prior experience with the feeling, but the feeling of utter rightness that settled around him told him he'd identified the emotion correctly.

He loved Ella.

But Ella didn't love him and didn't want to hang around to see if she might one day. This had to be some kind of cosmic punishment—karma, as Ella would say.

Karma sucked.

At least Ella got something out of all this. He could take away small comfort at being the subject of one of her paintings.

Her paintings…

Something niggled at the back of his mind. Something Ella had said about painting…

"All of those places are special to me. It's like I have an emotional attachment to them. I guess you could say I have to love it to paint it." She'd said it with a shrug, an offhand explanation for both her subject matter and why she kept all the canvases.

"I have to love it."

Knotting the towel around his hips, he headed for his bedroom. He pulled his laptop out of its briefcase, sat on the bed and waited impatiently for it to boot up. He logged in to his e-mail and ignored the ones from work as he scanned for Gillian's return address. She'd better have sent it…

There it was: "I could get fired for this. Don't spread it around—remember I know where you live."

Another click and *Fling* filled his screen, bringing a flood of memories now that the initial shock had passed. He didn't have time to reminisce, though; he was on a quest for answers. A closer look this time showed the unfinished aspects of the picture. Many of the details were missing, rough sketches where she planned to add to the background temporarily filling space.

But the man—him, for God's sake—was complete. He zoomed in, astounded by the detail. If he looked closely, he could see the fine shading that gave the muscles their definition and created the shallow line of his spine. He could almost count each and every hair on his head. If the digital image showed so much, he could only imagine the detail of the real thing.

But it was the glow around the man, caused by the play of light, that proved his case.

If she had to love what she painted, then she loved this man. Every tiny brushstroke showed the care and attention to detail only someone in love with the subject would take.

Ella loved him.

Then why had she pushed him away?

In that moment he decided he didn't care why. Ella loved him, and he loved her, and that was all that mattered. He'd do whatever he had to do to get her to admit it.

They would work the rest of the details out later.

He had the area code for south Alabama punched into the phone before he stopped himself. This wasn't exactly a conversation that would work well over the phone. *If* she even answered once she saw his name on the caller ID. Ella was trying to get away from this emotional tangle, so she'd probably avoid him at all costs—just like she did last weekend.

He sent an e-mail to his assistant, telling her he'd be out Monday and probably Tuesday, as well, and provided instructions for his current projects for the paralegals to take care of. That gave him three days to get through to Ella. Hopefully she wouldn't prove too stubborn about it. But if she were, at least his prime piece of evidence would be close by.

Showing up unannounced on her front porch again might get him arrested for attempted stalking, but it was the only plan he had at the moment. It wasn't much of a plan, granted, but he had a nice long drive to work out the details.

Feeling better than he had all week, he went to pack for the beach.

CHAPTER TWELVE

ELLA looked across at Ross as he cut the Jaguar's engine and silence replaced the low purr that had hummed under her feet on the way home from dinner. His interest in her at Melanie's house had proved genuine—even if she hadn't been in prime form that day—and he'd wasted no time in contacting her once back down south. An e-mail invitation to dinner was waiting in her in-box when she arrived home Monday afternoon. Thanks to her deal with her own personal she-devil, she'd felt honor bound to accept.

Big mistake.

Ross was cute, charming and funny. They had lots in common. He had a good job, a nice car and good personal hygiene. By all accounts, he was a prime catch. Her standards weren't artificially high.

But he wasn't Matt.

Worse, he was friends with Matt. And *that* was a big problem in more ways than she could count.

The fact Matt's name kept coming up at dinner didn't

help. Ross had known Matt and Brian since high school: a good number of his stories started with "The time Brian, Matt and I…" Each mention of Matt was like a knife in her heart. It wasn't exactly the best way to work on forgetting him. If anything, she was brooding worse than before.

Plus, dating one of Matt's friends—even if they weren't really close these days—just seemed wrong. And tacky.

Walking around to the passenger door, Ross opened it and assisted her out of the low-slung car. Completing the "prime catch" standards with good manners, he cupped his hand under her elbow and walked her to her front door. He waited as she slid her key into the lock and opened the door just a crack.

"I had a nice time tonight, Ross. Thank you."

"Me, too, Ella. And I hope we can do it again soon."

She smiled in what she hoped was a friendly, yet non-committal way. As he continued to stand there, she realized Ross hoped to be invited in. There was no way she was ready for that step.

"I'd invite you in, but I'm living in a construction zone at the moment…"

Thankfully Ross accepted the brush-off graciously. "Another time."

He leaned in to kiss her, and panic swelled in her chest. At the last second she turned and his lips brushed her cheek instead. Disappointment flashed in his eyes, but Ross was gallant enough not to mention it. Hopefully, he'd just think she was an old-fashioned kind of girl and not press his luck.

Relief washed over her as he squeezed her hand and said good-night instead. Then, with a smile that made her wish she wasn't in love with his friend, Ross headed back to his fancy car and drove away with a wave.

Ella released her breath and relaxed for the first time in hours. She hoped that bottle of wine in the fridge had a full glass still in it. After the past couple of hours, her nerves needed the balm only alcohol could provide.

She pushed against the door, and the hairs on her neck prickled as if someone was watching her. A movement in the shadows to her right caught her attention, and a short scream escaped as a man emerged from the shadows.

Roscoe, woofing loudly at her shriek, bounded off his porch and thundered across the street as his owner's porch light flipped on.

Matt spoke her name about the same instant she recognized him. A hundred emotions slammed into her at the sound of his voice, but she didn't have time to entertain any of them. A split second later Roscoe arrived at her side growling menacingly. Although still technically a puppy, he reached Ella's waist and weighed over a hundred pounds, and he placed himself between Ella and the man he considered a possible threat. Matt wisely stood still, waiting for the dog to calm down.

"Easy, boy," she said, rubbing his head gently. "It's okay." Not convinced, Roscoe moved closer to her, almost knocking her off her feet. The low growl kept

Matt where he stood, his eyes drilling into hers. He looked tired. And a bit peeved, for some reason. Although she wanted to be angry with him for showing up when she was trying to accept his absence, she wasn't. Well, not completely.

Roscoe's owner stepped out onto her porch calling, "Everything okay, Ella?"

"Everything's fine. I just got startled. Could you call Roscoe off, please?"

Roscoe, who took his job as neighborhood watchdog seriously, went home slowly, still woofing in Matt's general direction. He retreated to his doghouse but lay there watching Matt suspiciously.

Shaking a little from both the adrenaline and his presence, she released the energy on Matt. "You certainly know how to make an entrance, don't you? You're lucky Roscoe's more bark than bite."

"I'll keep that in mind."

She hated the way her voice shook, and she opened the door with more force than necessary. "What are you doing here, anyway?" She went inside without waiting for his answer, not inviting him in, but not closing the door in his face, either.

She really didn't want to deal with him right now. She was still reeling and dealing with raw emotions she didn't know how to handle, and a night with Ross and his trips down memory lane starring Matt hadn't exactly put her in the proper mind-set for this encounter.

But she couldn't leave him standing on the porch,

either—especially since they'd supposedly cleared the air between them last week—so she waved him in when he hovered in the doorway. "Well?"

"I wanted to talk to you," Matt muttered, seeming uncomfortable.

"You could have just called."

"But would you have answered?" The cheeky challenge made her want to smack him.

She shrugged before turning to search the fridge for that wine. Relaxing was now out of the question, but steadying would be nice. "Why wouldn't I? We both apologized for before, and I don't hold grudges."

But she *was* having a hard time holding down her dinner as her stomach roiled. She hoped her voice sounded normal, or, if not, at least could be chalked up to the scare. "Would you like some wine?" When he declined, she pushed forward. "Okay, then, talk to me. I'm listening."

Matt watched her closely as she poured her wine, and his silent stare frayed what was left of her nerves. She took deep breaths to keep her temper from flaring up, and aimed for a casual tone. "Well?"

"You look like you're feeling better."

Okay, small talk it is. And while she knew they were both avoiding something bigger—whatever it might be—it did give her the chance to mentally regroup. "I am, thanks. Fully recovered."

"Good."

She was going to scream if he didn't quit staring and

say something. The suspense was killing her, but she'd be damned if she'd ask him again to—

"Please tell me that wasn't really Ross Kelly dropping you off."

Her head spun at the sudden change of topic. Dare she hope that was jealousy she heard in his voice? "Do you want me to lie?"

"You're dating one of my friends? I can't believe it." The edge of his voice could cut glass, and she took a deep breath to keep herself from recoiling.

"We had dinner. He's a very nice guy. Not that it's any of *your* business, mind you."

"Oh, I think it is my business." With an exasperated noise, Matt caught her hand, pulled her around the counter to the other side and sat her on a bar stool. Instead of taking the other for himself, he stood in front of her, hands braced on his hips. "Ross Kelly is a mama's boy who—"

She wanted to scream in frustration. "Honestly, Matt. Am I supposed to believe you drove all the way down here to insult my choice in dinner companions?"

Matt simply raised an eyebrow at her.

"I didn't think so." Okay, so she was being combative and juvenile, but offense seemed the best defense at the moment. "Why don't you just say whatever it was you came to say—"

"You are the most infuriating, frustrating woman I've ever met. You're a distrustful control freak who keeps everyone at arm's length. You, Ella Mackenzie, are a serious trial to a man's patience."

His words felt like a slap, and though there was no heat in his voice, it didn't remove the sting. Anger quickly followed, though.

"Gee, you really know how to flatter a girl, don't you?" Too angry to sit still, she slid off the bar stool and paced. "Let me give you a helpful pointer or two, though. If you're wanting to get lucky, you might want to work on your pickup lines."

"I didn't come all the way down here for a quick lay." A small muscle in his jaw twitched, but otherwise his face was impassive. She knew better, though. She'd seen that look before. Whatever was going on, she wasn't going to like it one bit. The quicker she could brazen her way through this, the better. "Look, I apologized for how I acted before. So did you, so I don't see—"

"I saw the painting, Ella."

She froze in shock. *Oh, hell.* "What? When? *How?*"

Matt chuckled. "It's kinda nice to see you at a loss for words for once. Gillian's my neighbor, remember? She couldn't wait to thank me for sending you her way, and she thought *Fling* was a pretty good likeness. She says you're quite talented, by the way, and you should be hearing from her soon."

Excitement and pride over the professional assessment battled with the mortification of Matt seeing that painting. It was an odd feeling. Words really did escape her this time, and all she could manage was a small, "Oh."

"That's all you have to say?"

Good Lord, what *could* she say?

Matt's attention shifted to the easel sitting by the window, and her heart jumped into double time when he crossed the room and pulled off the sheet.

She bit her lip, wondering if it was possible to actually die of embarrassment as he studied the painting carefully.

"It's even more impressive in person. You're good, El. Subject matter aside, I can see why Gillian's excited about this one. The *chiro...cior*—"

"*Chiaroscuro,*" she supplied automatically.

"Whatever it is, you're good at it." His eyes pinned hers. "You should have told me."

She sorted through possible explanations and discarded them all as lame. "Um, I guess I should apologize for putting that painting out there without your permission. I just wanted to send something different— along with the landscapes, I mean. Something to show I could do more than watercolors and landscapes. It's not even finished, so I'm sure I can pull it from consideration pretty easily." Matt kept staring, and she wanted the sand dunes outside to come bury her. He'd missed his true calling by going into contract law. He should be in court, shredding witnesses on cross-examination. "I didn't think about the possibility of her recognizing you. Honestly."

"That's not what I'm talking about, and I'm sure you know it. Hey, you're blushing." Finally bending a little, Matt took her hand and led her to the couch. This time he sat with her. His voice dropped a notch. "I just want to know if it's true."

"True?" She stalled, as she racked her brain for possibilities.

"I know I hit my head pretty hard that day, but I distinctly remember you saying you were picky about your subjects. You had to love it in order to paint it. Does that extend to me and my painting?"

Oh, hell. She was trapped. Matt had a knowing gleam in his eye, and for a moment she considered the consequences of a lie. Would he simply accept a denial and go back home? Was this some sort of strange game where he got even with her by getting her to confess to her feelings and leaving, anyway? Admitting she loved him was setting herself up to...to...

"Well, Ella?"

The smug challenge in his voice pushed her over the line, and she let her temper take the lead. "Yes, damn it, it's true. I fell in love with you, and now this whole thing is a giant mess. There. I said it. Are you happy now?" She met his eyes, fully intending to stare him down, but the bright glow she saw there stopped her temper in its tracks.

"Oh, yes." The corner of his mouth curved up. Reaching for her, he easily maneuvered her into his lap, and her entire body awoke with a loud cheer. When one hand curved around her cheek, her heart accelerated. "Very much so."

With those words, though, the familiar panic settled into her chest. As much as she might want to, she couldn't do this. All the pain, all the misery, all the confusion she'd suffered through the past few weeks had only strengthened her resolve that relationships weren't for her. Especially not with someone like Matt. Someone who completely—

As if reading her mind, Matt whispered, "Just trust me a little."

"I can't. I'd like to, but I just *can't*." It had hurt too badly the last time he left. She couldn't go through that again. And it would only be worse next time.

"Yes, you can."

The calm surety in his voice both irritated her and soothed her at the same time. It was too confusing and exactly the kind of unbalance she needed to avoid. "Matt, I—"

"You've got to let it go, Ella." His breath tickled the hairs at her temple, and as she inhaled, his scent coiled through her and calmed her. When he put his forehead to hers, caught her in his chocolate gaze and added, "I love you, too," the tight feeling in her chest loosened.

But old habits die hard. "But what about—"

"Relax. Everything else is details, and we'll work them out later. This is all that matters." His lips captured hers, and in that moment she believed him.

Matt's fingers threaded through her hair, massaging her scalp and fanning the tiny flame that had burned in her stomach since he arrived. She turned to face him, wrapping her legs around his waist as he sat.

"Tell me," he whispered.

"I love you."

As soon as she said it, Matt surged to his feet and unerringly covered the distance to her bedroom without ever breaking the kiss.

He laid her carefully on the bed, then stood to pull his shirt over his head, giving Ella a feeling of déjà vu. Only, this time she was looking forward to the "messy" part and everything that came after. Her control-freak nature rebelled, demanding contingency plans and escape routes, but she stomped it down. Going with the flow wasn't a bad thing—especially considering the company.

Matt joined her on the bed, his fingers working at the buttons on her dress. "I should feel bad, taking you away from a friend of mine. It's against the guy code."

She spread her hands against the hard planes of his chest, sighing as the energy from him flowed through her fingertips. "I only went out with Ross because I promised Mel I would."

"Remind me to kill Melanie the next time I see her."

She laughed at the heat in his voice. "No need. I don't think Ross will ask me out a second time. It's hard to date when you're in love with someone else." She gasped as his fingers tightened over the bare skin of her hip and pulled her closer to him.

"Glad to hear it."

"Even if I am bad-tempered and frustrating?"

Matt grinned. "Yep."

"Then I'm all yours."

He groaned as her hand moved lower and his lips found the side of her neck. "Good."

His slow exploration of her skin with his hands and mouth set her on fire, but Matt wouldn't be hurried. She moved restlessly against him until he circled her wrists with one hand and pinned them over her head. With one heavy thigh draped over her, she was unable to move. Matt's eyes bored into hers. "Tell me again."

"I love you, I love you, I love you."

To her immense pleasure, Matt showed her how much he appreciated her words.

EPILOGUE

"AND I'm saying, you can't take it to Gillian for the show." Matt turned mulish and placed himself between her and the canvas, which made it very difficult for Ella to put *Fling* in its crate.

"Are you kidding me? Did you not *see* the sale estimate she recommended? Plus she says it's going to be a highlight of the show."

"Choose one of the others instead. This one's mine."

"We don't have time for this." She tried to maneuver around him, but he stood like a brick wall between her and *Fling*. She tried a shove. "*Move. Fling* is going in the show."

They should have been on the road an hour ago, but Matt had a knack for distracting her. Gillian needed the canvases in Atlanta by tomorrow morning to start setting the March show.

It had taken Matt three weeks to talk her into going part-time—only three days a week—at SoftWerx, which he called an eternity but felt like warp speed to her. It had given her more time to paint, finishing *Fling* and starting work on another. He'd also talked her into usually spending the other four days a week in Atlanta, making her such a frequent visitor to the Pensacola airport in the past two months that she and the ticket agents and security guards were on a first-name basis now.

Now, after pushing her so hard to paint and to let Gillian sign her for this show, he'd decided to dig his heels in about not putting this particular painting on display. She should have declined his offer to come help her crate the canvases and drive her to Atlanta.

"It's *my* painting, and I say it's going."

"Then I'll buy it from you."

"Be serious."

"I am. Name your price."

Truth be told, she didn't want to actually sell *Fling*—and she'd told Gillian that already—but she did want it in the show. Matt didn't know that yet, and his obstinate attitude rankled her into *not* telling him.

The other thing Matt didn't know was that she'd finally decided to move to Atlanta after the show opened in mid-March. Her bosses had agreed to let her telecommute, so she could keep her SoftWerx security blanket, as Matt called it, for the time being. Matt seemed to understand her inability to let go all at once, so while he'd offered to be her personal patron of the arts so she could paint full-time, he didn't push too hard too soon.

Which was just another reason she loved him. Even if she still wanted to strangle him on occasion. Like now.

"I'm not selling you this painting."

Instead of launching a counterattack, Matt shifted course. "How about a trade instead?" The corners of his mouth twitched, daring her to accept.

"A trade? I'm intrigued."

"I'll trade this," he said, pulling a small black box from his pocket, "for that."

Her heart skipped a beat as he opened the box and a diamond winked at her. It was too soon. It was too much.

It was perfect.

"Well, Ella? What do you say?" Matt's grin crinkled the corners of his eyes as he held the box out to her.

"It's beautiful." And, as crazy as it sounded, she wanted to accept the ring and everything that might come with it. Maybe she could get that happily-ever-after thing herself.

"That's not what I asked."

You haven't actually asked me anything. But two could play that game. "I'm going to show *Fling*—but I never planned to sell it. And I won't trade for it, either. It's yours—*after* the show. No strings attached."

Matt pulled her close. "Oh, there are strings. Lots of them. And the first is that you'll need to give it a new name. We were never just a fling."

"I beg to differ. We were *supposed* to be a fling—in fact, it was your bright plan to start with, remember?"

"So even the best-laid plans work out differently than expected. Come on, Ella," he coaxed with a smile. "Do you want to get married?"

"Is that an offer or just a request for information?"

"This time it's definitely an offer."

She smiled and held out her hand. "Finally, the right guy asks me."

Matt wrapped her in an embrace that guaranteed they'd be at least another hour late getting on the road.

MILLS & BOON

JANUARY 2010 HARDBACK TITLES

ROMANCE

Untamed Billionaire, Undressed Virgin	Anna Cleary
Pleasure, Pregnancy and a Proposition	Heidi Rice
Exposed: Misbehaving with the Magnate	Kelly Hunter
Pregnant by the Playboy Tycoon	Anne Oliver
The Secret Mistress Arrangement	Kimberly Lang
The Marcolini Blackmail Marriage	Melanie Milburne
Bought: One Night, One Marriage	Natalie Anderson
Confessions of a Millionaire's Mistress	Robyn Grady
Housekeeper at His Beck and Call	Susan Stephens
Public Scandal, Private Mistress	Susan Napier
Surrender to the Playboy Sheikh	Kate Hardy
The Magnate's Indecent Proposal	Ally Blake
His Mistress, His Terms	Trish Wylie
The Boss's Bedroom Agenda	Nicola Marsh
Master of Mallarinka & Hired: His Personal Assistant	Way & Steele
The Lucchesi Bride & Adopted: One Baby	Winters & Oakley
An Italian Affair	Margaret McDonagh
Small Miracles	Jennifer Taylor

HISTORICAL

One Unashamed Night	Sophia James
The Captain's Mysterious Lady	Mary Nichols
The Major and the Pickpocket	Lucy Ashford

MEDICAL™

A Winter Bride	Meredith Webber
A Dedicated Lady	Gill Sanderson
An Unexpected Choice	Alison Roberts
Nice And Easy	Josie Metcalfe

1209 Gen Std LP

JANUARY 2010 LARGE PRINT TITLES

ROMANCE

Marchese's Forgotten Bride	Michelle Reid
The Brazilian Millionaire's Love-Child	Anne Mather
Powerful Greek, Unworldly Wife	Sarah Morgan
The Virgin Secretary's Impossible Boss	Carole Mortimer
Claimed: Secret Royal Son	Marion Lennox
Expecting Miracle Twins	Barbara Hannay
A Trip with the Tycoon	Nicola Marsh
Invitation to the Boss's Ball	Fiona Harper

HISTORICAL

The Piratical Miss Ravenhurst	Louise Allen
His Forbidden Liaison	Joanna Maitland
An Innocent Debutante in Hanover Square	Anne Herries

MEDICAL™

The Valtieri Marriage Deal	Caroline Anderson
The Rebel and the Baby Doctor	Joanna Neil
The Country Doctor's Daughter	Gill Sanderson
Surgeon Boss, Bachelor Dad	Lucy Clark
The Greek Doctor's Proposal	Molly Evans
Single Father: Wife and Mother Wanted	Sharon Archer

0110 Gen Std HB

™ MILLS & BOON®

FEBRUARY 2010 HARDBACK TITLES

ROMANCE

At the Boss's Beck and Call	Anna Cleary
Hot-Shot Tycoon, Indecent Proposal	Heidi Rice
Revealed: A Prince and A Pregnancy	Kelly Hunter
Hot Boss, Wicked Nights	Anne Oliver
The Millionaire's Misbehaving Mistress	Kimberly Lang
Between the Italian's Sheets	Natalie Anderson
Naughty Nights in the Millionaire's Mansion	Robyn Grady
Sheikh Boss, Hot Desert Nights	Susan Stephens
Bought: One Damsel in Distress	Lucy King
The Billionaire's Bought Mistress	Annie West
Playboy Boss, Pregnancy of Passion	Kate Hardy
A Night with the Society Playboy	Ally Blake
One Night with the Rebel Billionaire	Trish Wylie
Two Weeks in the Magnate's Bed	Nicola Marsh
Magnate's Mistress…Accidentally Pregnant	Kimberly Lang
Desert Prince, Blackmailed Bride	Kim Lawrence
The Nurse's Baby Miracle	Janice Lynn
Second Lover	Gill Sanderson

HISTORICAL

The Rake and the Heiress	Marguerite Kaye
Wicked Captain, Wayward Wife	Sarah Mallory
The Pirate's Willing Captive	Anne Herries

MEDICAL™

Angel's Christmas	Caroline Anderson
Someone To Trust	Jennifer Taylor
Morrison's Magic	Abigail Gordon
Wedding Bells	Meredith Webber

0110 Gen Std LP

FEBRUARY 2010 LARGE PRINT TITLES

ROMANCE

Desert Prince, Bride of Innocence	Lynne Graham
Raffaele: Taming His Tempestuous Virgin	Sandra Marton
The Italian Billionaire's Secretary Mistress	Sharon Kendrick
Bride, Bought and Paid For	Helen Bianchin
Betrothed: To the People's Prince	Marion Lennox
The Bridesmaid's Baby	Barbara Hannay
The Greek's Long-Lost Son	Rebecca Winters
His Housekeeper Bride	Melissa James

HISTORICAL

The Brigadier's Daughter	Catherine March
The Wicked Baron	Sarah Mallory
His Runaway Maiden	June Francis

MEDICAL™

Emergency: Wife Lost and Found	Carol Marinelli
A Special Kind of Family	Marion Lennox
Hot-Shot Surgeon, Cinderella Bride	Alison Roberts
A Summer Wedding at Willowmere	Abigail Gordon
Miracle: Twin Babies	Fiona Lowe
The Playboy Doctor Claims His Bride	Janice Lynn

millsandboon.co.uk Community

Join Us!

he Community is the perfect place to meet and chat to
indred spirits who love books and reading as much as you
o, but it's also the place to:

- Get the inside scoop from authors about their latest books
- Learn how to write a romance book with advice from our editors
- Help us to continue publishing the best in women's fiction
- Share your thoughts on the books we publish
- Befriend other users

orums: Interact with each other as well as authors, editors
nd a whole host of other users worldwide.

logs: Every registered community member has their own
log to tell the world what they're up to and what's on their
ind.

ook Challenge: We're aiming to read 5,000 books and
ave joined forces with The Reading Agency in our
augural Book Challenge.

rofile Page: Showcase yourself and keep a record of your
cent community activity.

ocial Networking: We've added buttons at the end of
very post to share via digg, Facebook, Google, Yahoo,
chnorati and de.licio.us.

www.millsandboon.co.uk